Alice-Miranda at Camp

Books by Jacqueline Harvey

Alice-Miranda at School
Alice-Miranda on Holiday
Alice-Miranda Takes the Lead
Alice-Miranda at Sea
Alice-Miranda in New York
Alice-Miranda Shows the Way
Alice-Miranda in Paris
Alice-Miranda Shines Bright
Alice-Miranda in Japan
Alice-Miranda at Camp

Clementine Rose and the Surprise Visitor
Clementine Rose and the Pet Day Disaster
Clementine Rose and the Perfect Present
Clementine Rose and the Farm Fiasco
Clementine Rose and the Seaside Escape
Clementine Rose and the Treasure Box

Alice-Miranda at Camp

Jacqueline Harvey

RANDOM HOUSE AUSTRALIA

A Random House book
Published by Random House Australia Pty Ltd
Level 3, 100 Pacific Highway, North Sydney NSW 2060
www.randomhouse.com.au

First published by Random House Australia in 2014

Addresses for companies within the Random House Group can be found at www.randomhouse.com.au/offices

National Library of Australia
Cataloguing-in-Publication Entry

Author: Harvey, Jacqueline
Title: Alice-Miranda at camp/Jacqueline Harvey
ISBN: 978 1 74275 761 2 (paperback)
Series: Harvey, Jacqueline. Alice-Miranda; 10
Target audience: For primary school age
Subjects: School camps – Juvenile fiction
Boarding schools – Juvenile fiction
Friendships – Juvenile fiction
Dewey number: A823.4

Cover and internal illustrations by J.Yi
Cover design by Mathematics www.xy-1.com
Internal design by Midland Typesetters, Australia
Typeset in 13/18 pt Adobe Garamond by Midland Typesetters, Australia
Printed in Australia by Griffin Press, an accredited ISO AS/NZS 14001:2004 Environmental Management System printer

Random House Australia uses papers that are natural, renewable and recyclable products and made from wood grown in sustainable forests. The logging and manufacturing processes are expected to conform to the environmental regulations of the country of origin.

For Ian, who made one school camp
especially memorable, and for Sandy,
who would love that we've come so far.

Prologue

The grandfather clock chimed two as the man made his way along the empty corridor towards the back staircase. Dust danced on the moonbeams that shone through the window at the end of the hall, lighting his path. Somewhere in the inky darkness outside a beast howled, but the house and its occupants slept on.

When he reached the ground floor, the man entered the disused kitchen. He passed the ancient cooker and empty cupboards and went through the butler's pantry to a locked door. He fumbled about in his dressing-gown pocket, retrieved a key and turned it in the lock. Then he closed the door behind him, pressed the button on the tiny torch in his other hand and walked down, down, down until another door blocked his path. This one required a different key. A moment later, safely on the other side, he flicked the switch on the wall.

A golden glow lit the space around him.

'Good evening, Sidney.' He nodded at the polar bear. The giant taxidermied beast stood guard over a jumble of antiques and household goods that had long ago been banished to the cellars. The man wove his way through the cast-offs, acknowledging several more trophy creatures. In the far corner of the room he pulled aside a thick black curtain to reveal a large metal door. With his glasses perched on the tip of his nose, he leaned down and turned the circular lock, listening for the clicks. One, eight, six, four. As he pulled on the handle, a blast of cool air escaped. He reached around and flicked a switch, then waited as a bank of fluorescent lights stuttered to life.

Inside, the vault walls were a jigsaw of paintings in heavily gilded frames. On the floor, rows upon rows of V-shaped racks contained yet more, smaller treasures. He shuffled past several racks before something caught his eye. He wondered why it seemed so out of place. His once-sharp memories often felt as blurred as the Impressionist landscapes he loved so much, but surely this was just his weary mind playing tricks. He shook his head, trying to focus, then looked across and spotted what he was searching for.

He lifted the painting out and propped it on the lone easel in the room.

The folding chair was hidden in an alcove, just as he'd left it. With its faded stripes and worn seat, its picnic days were a distant memory. He positioned the chair in front of the painting then sat down and stared into the glowing canvas. JMW Turner's landscapes had always been his favourite.

He pulled a chocolate from his pocket and slowly peeled the golden wrapper. As he popped the confection into his mouth, he didn't notice the foil flutter to the floor.

Minutes became an hour and the alarm on his watch beeped. He returned the chair to its original position and the painting to its rack.

Back in the cellar, he pulled the vault door and spun the dial, then retraced his steps up to the butler's pantry, locking the doors behind him. He stepped carefully across the kitchen flagstones, climbed the back stairs, and walked silently to his apartment, avoiding the squeaky floor boards that might rouse his slumbering neighbours. Then he climbed into bed and fell into a deep, deep sleep.

Chapter 1

As Alice-Miranda and Millie approached the music room on their way to afternoon tea, they heard the most extraordinary sound. A voice, as smooth as honey and just as rich, floated into the hallway.

'Is that Jacinta?' Millie asked.

Alice-Miranda shook her head. 'No, wouldn't she be at Caledonia Manor with the year sevens?'

Millie nodded. 'I suppose so, but it doesn't sound like Sloane either. It must be one of the new girls. What a voice! They'll definitely hate her, you know.'

'Who'll hate her?' Alice-Miranda asked.

'Jacinta and Sloane, of course,' said Millie.

Alice-Miranda grinned. 'Millie, you know that's not true. But I think Mr Lipp's going to want whoever it is in the choir.'

Just as the girls reached the open door, the soloist stopped. Alice-Miranda and Millie peeked into the room.

Mr Trout was sitting at the grand piano clasping his hands together. 'Bravo, my dear. That was beautiful, absolutely beautiful!'

Miss Reedy was standing beside him. A tall girl had her back to the door. 'Is that the piece you sang for the National Eisteddfod?' the English teacher asked.

'Yes,' the girl replied with a nod.

Mr Trout beamed. 'What an accomplishment to win the open category at your age.'

The girl shrugged.

Miss Reedy glanced over at the doorway and spotted Alice-Miranda and Millie. 'Oh girls, perfect timing. Come and meet Caprice Radford.'

The pair hurried into the room as the willowy girl turned and looked at them. She had a long mane of copper-coloured hair, with a blunt fringe framing sparkling sapphire-blue eyes. Her pale skin was luminous and Alice-Miranda thought she was probably about ten or eleven years old.

Alice-Miranda stepped forward and held out her hand. 'Hello, my name's Alice-Miranda Highton-Smith-Kennington-Jones and I'm very pleased to meet you.'

'I'm Caprice Radford,' the girl replied. She reached out and gave Alice-Miranda's hand a shake as limp as a fish.

The group looked expectantly at Millie, who for a moment seemed to have fallen under some sort of hypnotic spell.

'Oh, me?' the girl blathered. 'I'm just Millie.' She hadn't meant to stare but the newcomer was ridiculously pretty.

'Hi,' Caprice said, looking the flame-haired child up and down.

'Caprice arrived after lunch and we've been having a tour of the school. It was fortunate that we ran into Mr Trout and Caprice told him about her singing. I don't know if you heard any of it, but she's marvellous,' Miss Reedy gasped.

Alice-Miranda and Millie nodded. 'Yes, we heard,' Alice-Miranda said.

'Girls, would you please take Caprice to afternoon tea and then to the boarding house?' asked Miss Reedy. 'Mr Trout and I have a meeting to attend.'

'Of course, Miss Reedy,' Alice-Miranda replied. She paused, frowning. 'Oh. I just remembered I have to collect a sports shirt from Miss Wall. Millie, could you take Caprice and I'll meet you there in a minute?'

'Sure,' Millie said as Alice-Miranda shot off.

'Thanks, girls. We'll see you later,' Miss Reedy said.

Caprice followed Millie to the door then turned and smiled at the teachers. 'I'm really looking forward to singing in the choir, Mr Trout. Please keep me in mind for some of the solos if you think I might be good enough.' She fluttered her long eyelashes.

'Oh, absolutely.' Cornelius Trout felt a tingle run the length of his spine. He couldn't remember ever hearing such a prodigious talent before.

'What a charming girl,' Miss Reedy said loudly.

'Yes, indeed,' Mr Trout agreed.

A smug smile settled on Caprice's face as she joined Millie in the corridor. The two girls walked to the door at the end of the hallway and out into the sunny courtyard.

'Do you have singing lessons?' Millie asked.

'No,' Caprice replied sharply.

'Really? Your voice is amazing,' said Millie.

'Everyone says that,' Caprice said matter-of-factly. 'It gets *so* boring after a while.'

'I don't think it would be boring to be able to sing like you,' Millie said.

Caprice shot Millie a pitying stare. 'I guess you'll never know.'

Millie looked at the girl. What she said was true, but considering Caprice had never heard her sing, it seemed an odd thing to say.

'The dining room's over there.' Millie pointed at the freshly painted blue door.

The place was buzzing with students swapping stories of their holidays and moaning about the amount of work some of their teachers had already set. After all, they'd only arrived back yesterday and today was the first day of lessons. The pair joined the end of the long line at the servery.

'Where did you go to school before here?' Millie asked.

'Lots of places,' Caprice replied.

Millie wondered what that meant. 'Did your parents move around a lot?'

'No,' Caprice snapped. 'Why would you think that?'

Millie wondered what she'd said to upset her. The girl's sunny nature seemed to have turned decidedly dark.

'Why did you change schools then?' Millie asked.

'You ask a lot of questions. If you must know, I won the academic scholarship, and the work at my old schools was always way too easy. Miss Grimm promised that I could do my lessons with the older girls so I don't get bored, but I probably will.'

'Alice-Miranda does a lot of extension work,' Millie said.

'Does she have a scholarship too?' Caprice asked.

Millie shook her head.

'Well, she can't be that smart then,' Caprice scoffed.

'Yes, she is,' Millie retorted. She was growing wary of this beautiful and 'brilliant' new student. 'Alice-Miranda is the smartest girl in the whole school.'

'Really? We'll see about that.' Caprice folded her arms and turned her back.

Chapter 2

Alice-Miranda scooted in beside Millie just as the girls arrived in front of the food. The servery was dotted with plates bearing thick wedges of cake covered in sticky white frosting.

'Sorry, I couldn't find Miss Wall,' the child puffed. She noticed that Millie's face was as dark as the gathering thunderclouds outside and Caprice was staring off into the distance.

'Is everything all right?' Alice-Miranda asked. She wondered what had happened in the past ten minutes.

Millie plastered on a fake smile but it was clear to Alice-Miranda that something had gone wrong.

'Hello Mrs Smith,' Alice-Miranda greeted the cook. 'This is Caprice. She just started today.'

Doreen Smith gave a pinched smile and nodded in the children's direction, then wiped her shiny forehead with the back of her hand. Her face was tomato red and there were dark circles under her eyes.

'Hello dear,' the old woman sighed.

Caprice swivelled around. Her taut expression softened. 'Hello Mrs Smith,' she replied with a beguiling smile.

Millie looked up, surprised by the change in Caprice's voice.

'Are you all right, Mrs Smith?' Alice-Miranda asked. 'You don't look well.'

The woman exhaled loudly. 'I hadn't realised that cooking for an extra twenty-five children and a few new teachers would be like cooking for an extra hundred and twenty-five. And now the big cooker is on the blink and I'm trying to manage with the old range. It's a disaster.'

'Oh dear, that's no good at all,' Alice-Miranda said. She glanced around. The queue of girls was gone and the teachers were helping themselves. 'Can you sit down for a minute? I could bring you a cup of tea.'

'That would be heavenly, sweetheart. Charlie's out chopping wood for me now. Who'd have thought I'd be back to wood-fired cooking? But I suppose I should thank my lucky stars that we still have the old girl. It would be toast for tea tonight otherwise.' Mrs Smith continued muttering to herself, bubbling and hissing like a boiling pot as she walked out from behind the counter and sat at a nearby table.

Alice-Miranda passed Millie two plates of hummingbird cake and handed Caprice another two before darting off to make Mrs Smith's tea.

Millie put the cakes down on the table with a thud. Caprice sat opposite her, beside Mrs Smith.

A minute later, Alice-Miranda joined them, placing a cup of tea in front of the exhausted woman. 'How long will you have to cook for the older girls as well, Mrs Smith?'

'At least a couple of weeks. I know Miss Grimm had hoped everything would be finished in time for the start of school but this bleak weather has done the builders no favours,' Mrs Smith explained.

'It will be so strange when the older girls move,' Alice-Miranda said. 'At the moment it still feels the same, although there are extra beds everywhere in Grimthorpe House and the queue for the showers this morning was all the way down the hall.'

'Why?' Caprice asked.

'The school's just expanded into year seven but the senior campus is at Caledonia Manor, which is on the other side of the woods. Their boarding house isn't ready yet so everyone's bunking in together at Grimthorpe House until the girls can move,' said Alice-Miranda.

'You should see the place,' Millie added. 'It's a nightmare and Mrs Howard looks as tired as Mrs Smith, even with Shaker helping out.' The girl paused. 'Actually, she probably looks that way *because* of Shaker helping out.'

'Get off, you cheeky moppet.' Mrs Smith grinned and rolled her eyes. 'Shaker's a lovely old thing – even if she does seem to forget more than she remembers some days.'

'So will I have to share a room?' Caprice asked.

'We all do,' Millie scoffed. 'It's not a hotel, you know.'

'Millie!' Alice-Miranda was surprised by the tone of her friend's voice. 'It won't be for long, Caprice. I'm not sure where you'll be sleeping but you might have to share with two girls instead of just one until the building work is done.'

'Nobody told me that.' Caprice pressed her lips tightly together.

'We don't have any extra beds in our room,' Millie said and raised her eyebrows ever so slightly. Caprice glared back across the table.

'Miss Grimm didn't say anything about the school development when Mummy and I met with her last year,' Caprice said. 'I told Mummy I should have gone to Sainsbury Palace instead.'

'Miss Grimm only decided to add year seven at the last minute,' Alice-Miranda explained. 'And believe me, I'm sure you'll be much happier here.' She wasn't about to go into details about what had happened when Jacinta went to the Sainsbury Palace Orientation Day, but it seemed Millie had other ideas.

'What a pity you didn't go there – Mrs Jelly and Professor Crookston are *so* lovely. And I'm sure that they would have been thrilled to have such a talented student,' Millie said.

Mrs Smith and Alice-Miranda looked at Millie, wondering what she was talking about. Everyone knew that Miss Grimm had decided to expand the school after Jacinta had her terrible run-in with Professor Crookston and Mildred Jelly defended his horrid behaviour.

'That's true,' Caprice agreed. 'But Mummy insisted that I take the scholarship here.'

'I'm sure the boarding house will be sorted soon enough.' Mrs Smith sighed again then took a sip of her tea.

'This cake is delicious,' Alice-Miranda said, changing the subject.

'I'm glad you like it, dear,' the woman replied. 'It's Venetia Baldini's recipe.'

On hearing the woman's name, Caprice looked up.

'How many hummingbirds did you have to sacrifice for this one?' Millie said with a grin. She stabbed her fork into the thick wedge of cake and gobbled a chunk down.

Alice-Miranda and Mrs Smith chortled.

Caprice frowned.

'It's a joke,' Millie said. 'There aren't really any hummingbirds in hummingbird cake.'

'I know that!' Caprice snapped. 'It's my mother's recipe.'

Millie sputtered cake crumbs all over the table. 'Your mother?'

'Yes,' Caprice nodded. 'My mother *is* Venetia Baldini.'

'Oh, heavens,' Mrs Smith said. 'The woman's a genius.'

Millie shook her head. 'Well, I've never heard of her.' But that wasn't completely true. The name was familiar. Millie wondered if she was the beautiful woman her grandfather liked to watch on television.

'Ms Baldini's very famous,' Alice-Miranda explained. 'Mrs Oliver and Shilly never miss an episode of *Sweet Things*. And I know Mrs Oliver has tried lots of your mother's recipes too. I love her honey jumbles – they're the best ever.'

'And Venetia's such a sweet woman,' Mrs Smith agreed.

If that were true, Millie wondered what had happened to her daughter.

Mrs Smith glanced at the clock. 'Oop! I'd better get on with dinner.' She pushed her chair back and thanked Alice-Miranda for the tea then disappeared through the kitchen door.

'We'd better get going too.' Alice-Miranda glanced around the near-empty room. 'I've got homework and I want to go and see how Bonaparte's settling in before dinner.'

'Who's that?' Caprice asked.

'He's my pony. He's very naughty but he's adorable,' Alice-Miranda explained.

'I have a Lipizzaner,' Caprice said.

Millie rolled her eyes.

'Oh, how gorgeous. Is he coming to school?' Alice-Miranda asked.

Caprice shook her head. 'He's far too valuable to bring here. We've got someone looking after him. He has to be ridden all the time.'

'Do you compete?' Alice-Miranda asked.

'We've won every single event we've entered,' Caprice said.

Millie was listening but pretending not to. You could have put a penguin on a properly trained Lipizzaner and they'd win, she thought to herself. It was her favourite breed of horse but she wasn't about to say so.

'What's his name?' Alice-Miranda asked.

'Shah,' Caprice replied.

'That's a great name. Isn't it, Millie?' the child said.

'Sorry, what did you say?' Millie looked vaguely at the pair.

'Shah. It's a great name for a horse,' Alice-Miranda repeated.

'Perfect,' said Millie. 'Just like its owner,' she whispered under her breath.

'What was that?' Caprice glared at Millie.

'Nothing,' the girl replied.

But Alice-Miranda had heard it too. She had a strange feeling and wanted to talk to Millie in private as soon as she could. Something clearly wasn't right.

'Well, we'd better go or Howie will send a search party.' Alice-Miranda stood up and took the three empty plates to the trolley at the end of the servery.

'Don't you like it?' Millie looked at the slab of cake left on Caprice's plate. The girl had barely touched it.

'Not really,' Caprice replied.

'I suppose you must eat lots of cake,' Millie said.

'Do I look like I eat a lot of cake?' Caprice spat.

'No, I didn't mean it like that. I just thought that if your mother's a chef and this is one of her recipes –' Millie began.

'You don't know anything about me, or my mother,' said Caprice, curling her lip. She stood up, leaving her plate on the table, and stalked off towards the door.

'We have to clear up after ourselves here,' Millie called. 'There are no servants.'

Caprice turned around. 'I'm sure you don't mind doing it for me. I mean, it's my first day and I don't know how anything works.'

She strode away to the door, where Alice-Miranda was talking to a teacher.

Millie could feel her anger rising. She took a deep breath, picked up the plate and fork beside it, and dumped them onto the tray with a noisy crash.

Chapter 3

Alice-Miranda, Millie and Caprice arrived at Grimthorpe House to find the place under siege from Mrs Howard, who seemed to be under siege from Shaker. The housemistress was on a mission to get the place in order, which was no small task given the addition of twenty-five girls and all their belongings.

'Good afternoon, Mrs Howard,' Alice-Miranda greeted the woman. She was almost bowled over by Susannah, who was carrying a tower of towels to the linen cupboard. Several other girls were heaving suitcases and boxes of books. 'This is Caprice.'

'Oh, welcome dear,' Mrs Howard told the girl. 'I've been expecting you. What a pity you weren't able to arrive yesterday with everyone else.'

'I'm sorry about that,' Caprice apologised. 'Mummy was recording a show and she needed all of the family to be there.'

'Yes, I met her this afternoon when she dropped your bags off and she told me so. Charming woman, and I do love watching *Sweet Things*.' Mrs Howard patted her stomach. 'You can see I like eating them even more. Anyway, never mind. This place seems twice as chaotic as yesterday, so you'll just have to cope, I'm afraid.'

'Would you like us to show Caprice to her room, Mrs Howard?' Alice-Miranda offered.

'Yes, please. Caprice is sharing with Jacinta and Sloane.'

Millie's stomach twisted. That sounded like a very bad idea. Jacinta and Sloane were fiery enough on their own at times without adding Little Miss Perfect to the mix.

Mrs Howard turned to Caprice. 'There's a chest of drawers for you, dear, and I've cleared the end of one wardrobe but I'm afraid you'll have to do your homework out here in the sitting room until Jacinta moves over to Caledonia Manor. Has anyone seen Sloane? She should have been back by now,' Mrs Howard quizzed. 'Actually, Millie, Alice-Miranda can take Caprice and you can stay here and help me with some jobs.'

'Why me?' Millie complained.

Howie glared. 'Why not you?'

'Yes, why not you?' Shaker's trembly voice echoed over the housemistress's shoulder.

Mrs Howard spun around. 'Oh, there you are, Mrs Shakeshaft. I need you to go and see how the new girls are getting on upstairs.'

'But I'd much rather help down here.'

Mrs Howard eyed the old woman. 'Are those cake crumbs around your mouth? You'd better not have been eating my supper.'

A sheepish look spread across Shaker's powdered face. She quickly brushed her lip and scuttled away down the hall.

'I'll come back and help in a minute,' Alice-Miranda said to Millie.

'Thanks,' the girl mouthed in reply.

Alice-Miranda led the way down the hall, pointing out who slept where and the bathroom on the right. 'This is it. Millie and I are next door.'

She turned the handle of Sloane and Jacinta's room and wondered what sort of state she'd find the place in. Neither of the girls was tidy and they spent most of the time blaming each other for the mess.

A third bed had been installed over the holidays. Alice-Miranda showed Caprice the spare chest of drawers and opened the door of Jacinta's wardrobe, glad that the usual avalanche of belongings stayed put.

'This is the hanging space Mrs Howard was talking about,' Alice-Miranda said.

Two suitcases and a giant tuck box sat at the foot of the new bed.

'Do you have room inspections?' Caprice asked.

Alice-Miranda nodded. 'Mrs Howard does them every week but she never tells us when they'll be.'

'What do you get if you win?' Caprice asked.

'All sorts of things. It's different every time. Sometimes the girls who win get to choose a place to go for a weekend outing or Mrs Smith makes their favourite treat. Last year Millie and I got to have afternoon tea with Miss Grimm in her study,' Alice-Miranda explained. 'It's always something lovely.'

'How many times has this room won?' Caprice asked.

The tiny child frowned. 'Mmm.' Alice-Miranda thought for a moment. 'Never.'

'Never! We'll see about that.' Caprice unzipped her first suitcase and flew into action.

'Do you want some help?' Alice-Miranda offered, grinning. Maybe Caprice was just what Jacinta and Sloane needed. Mrs Howard would be very grateful to have a tidy influence on the pair.

Caprice didn't look up. 'No, I'm fine.'

'I'll see you later then. Have fun with your unpacking.'

Alice-Miranda scurried down the hallway to the sitting room at the back of the house. Millie appeared from the utility room. The rest of the girls had disappeared and so had Mrs Howard and Shaker.

'What were you doing?' Alice-Miranda asked.

'I just had to carry some junk down to the cellar.'

The room was still crowded with boxes but neither girl knew what else Mrs Howard wanted moved.

'Come on, let's go before Howie comes back and gives us any more jobs. I've got homework,' said Millie.

'What happened before, with you and Caprice in the dining room?' Alice-Miranda asked.

'That girl's weird,' Millie said.

'What do you mean?'

'Well, one minute she was all sweet and lovely and then the next she was awful. I suppose it had to happen. We were always going to get a new one.'

Alice-Miranda shot Millie a curious look.

'A new Alethea. For a while it looked like Sloane would take that crown but she's not half as bad as she used to be,' Millie huffed.

'Sloane's fine and maybe Caprice is nervous about being at a new school,' Alice-Miranda said. 'What did she say to you?'

'She was showing off about winning the academic scholarship and she said that you weren't the cleverest girl in the school,' Millie said. 'She's so pretty too. You wait. She'll have the teachers wrapped around her little finger in no time.'

Alice-Miranda put her arm around Millie's shoulder. 'Don't be upset. I'm sure she's nothing like Alethea. And, you know, even she's changed a lot since she was here. Besides, I'm not the cleverest girl in the school.'

'Yes, you are. Anyway, I don't want to spend any more time with Caprice than I have to. I might catch something, like show-off's disease. I hear that's not very pleasant at all. Your head gets really, really big and you start shooting your mouth off about everything!'

Alice-Miranda frowned. Caprice had seemed fine to her and it wasn't like Millie to be jealous. There had to be more to it.

Chapter 4

'What a day!' Sloane moaned as she pushed open the door to her bedroom. She walked inside and did a double take, before backing out again to check that she was in the right place.

'Hey Millie, Alice-Miranda, are you there?' Sloane called from the hallway.

Millie flung open the door and looked out. Sloane was standing against the opposite wall with a puzzled look on her face.

'What's wrong?' Millie asked as Alice-Miranda appeared beside her.

'I just had to check.'

'Check what?' Millie asked.

'That I wasn't dreaming,' Sloane said, rubbing her eyes.

Alice-Miranda frowned. 'What are you talking about?'

'You have to see this.' Sloane scooted back through her bedroom door. The other girls followed.

'Whoa!' Millie gasped. 'What happened in here?'

Sloane shrugged. 'That's what I wanted to know.'

Alice-Miranda glanced around the room and smiled. Books were lined perfectly on the shelves according to height, ornaments were displayed as if they were in a shop window and three beautiful blue-and-white wallpaper prints adorned the walls above each of the beds. The third bed looked as if it was about to be photographed for a magazine – two plump blue cushions were propped against the pillows on a smart white duvet.

'Who did this?' Sloane asked.

'I think you've been Capriced,' Alice-Miranda said. 'I gather you haven't met your new roommate yet. I showed her in here a little while ago and when she started to unpack I knew she meant business. I didn't realise she'd go this far.'

Sloane opened the wardrobe. 'Are you kidding me? This too?'

Her clothes were lined up in order with dresses at the end, followed by skirts, pants and blouses.

Millie's face contorted. 'What sort of a weirdo does that?'

'I love her!' Sloane said.

'I think it had something to do with her asking me about room inspections,' said Alice-Miranda.

'Did you tell her Jacinta and I have never won?' Sloane asked.

Alice-Miranda nodded.

Sloane shrugged. 'I don't mind if she wants to tidy up. I'd love to win.'

But Alice-Miranda wondered if Millie wasn't just a little bit right. It did seem somewhat extreme. Alice-Miranda was renowned for her tidiness too but she wouldn't have dreamed of touching the other girls' things without asking.

'Sloane, are you there?' came a voice from the hall. It was Mrs Howard. The woman strode into the room. 'Good heavens, what happened in here?' Mrs Howard's eyes almost popped out of her head.

'Do you like it? I've been tidying up,' Sloane said, attempting to keep a straight face.

Mrs Howard glared at her. 'And I'm Queen Georgiana's long-lost sister.'

'Really?' Sloane looked at the woman. 'Good for you.'

Millie and Alice-Miranda giggled.

'Oh, all right. Caprice did it,' Sloane admitted.

'Do you know where I can get twenty more just like her?' Mrs Howard said with a smile.

'What a horrible thought,' Millie mumbled to herself.

'What was that, Millicent?' Mrs Howard asked.

She shook her head. 'Nothing.'

'Well, if you want to thank Caprice, she's out in the sitting room creating some of the most beautiful title pages I've ever seen,' Mrs Howard said. She held up the fabric that had been slung over her shoulder and waved it at Sloane. 'And I've just fixed your tunic. I suggest you stop growing, Sloane Sykes, or you'll be needing another uniform before the end of term.' She found a spare hanger in the wardrobe.

'Thanks,' Sloane said.

'I couldn't have you going around with staples holding up your hem, could I?' Mrs Howard tutted. 'Besides, they'd soon ruin the washing machine.'

Sloane grinned at Millie and Alice-Miranda. 'Sorry, sewing's not really Mummy's thing. I'll get changed and then I'll go and see Caprice.'

'If anyone needs me, I'm popping over to see Mrs Smith. Poor Doreen's in a bit of a muddle and I want to see if I can help her with dinner,' Mrs Howard said as she headed for the door. 'Oh, and the year seven girls are walking back from Caledonia Manor. Charlie went to get them but the bus broke down halfway between.'

'At least it's not raining,' Alice-Miranda said.

'Well, there is that.' Mrs Howard gave a wave and disappeared into the hall.

'I'd better get back and finish my story for Miss Reedy,' Alice-Miranda said.

'Do you want a drink?' Millie asked. 'Science homework always makes me thirsty.'

Alice-Miranda shook her head. 'I'm fine.'

'Not me,' Sloane said. 'But thanks.'

Alice-Miranda went back to their room and Millie walked out to the kitchenette, which was off the back sitting room. She expected to see Caprice doing her perfect title pages but the large table that had been brought into the house for the new girls to do their homework at was empty.

As she rounded the corner to the fridge, Millie heard a muffled voice.

It sounded like it was coming from the cupboard under the back stairs. She wondered who was hiding in there already. It was a favourite spot, especially when the girls wanted to steer clear of Mrs Howard and her jobs.

'You didn't tell me that I'd have to share a room, Mummy,' the voice hissed.

Millie knew immediately who it was.

'And it's a pigsty. I can't believe it – they've never ever won a room inspection.'

'Boo hoo,' Millie whispered, and made a face.

'And there's a horrible girl.'

Millie's eyes widened and she leaned closer to the door.

'She has red hair and freckles and she's ugly and mean. She said that I wasn't the cleverest girl in the school. She said that Alice-Miranda is and she's not. She's stupid and she's a baby,' Caprice spat.

Millie's jaw dropped.

There was a long silence.

'Don't tell me I'd better make the best of it. What! Well, you can tell Daddy that if he sells Shah I'll never speak to him again,' Caprice threatened.

Millie's stomach twisted. If Caprice's father had any sense at all that's exactly what he'd do.

'I hate you. And I hate Daddy.' A noise like a whimpering puppy came from the cupboard. The door flew open and Caprice stormed out.

Millie stared at her and took a deep breath. 'I heard what you said about me.'

'So now you're an eavesdropper too.' Caprice walked into the sitting room and slammed the telephone back into its cradle.

Millie followed her. 'It's not okay, you know!'

Caprice walked to the table where her books were piled neatly on top of one another. She ignored Millie completely.

An uncomfortable silence settled over the room.

The girl's poisonous words swirled in Millie's head. 'Calling someone mean and ugly isn't very nice, Caprice,' Millie persisted.

'I didn't say that,' Caprice lied.

'You must think I'm deaf and stupid,' Millie said with a gulp. She was determined not to cry.

Caprice's eyes filled with tears. 'You made *me* feel stupid.'

'What?' Millie couldn't believe what she was hearing. 'Why are you crying? You're the one who's mean. You're just upset because I heard you.'

'You don't understand what it's like. I'm new and I don't know anything and all anyone cares about is my famous mother.' Caprice's shoulders began to heave.

The girl deserved an Academy Award, Millie thought to herself. She brushed away the fat tears that had spilled onto her cheeks and glanced around for a box of tissues.

Sloane walked into the room. She looked at Millie and then at the new girl, who she assumed was Caprice.

'What's the matter?' she asked, rushing to Caprice's side.

Millie shook her head and dumped a handful of tissues on the table in front of Caprice.

The girl took them, then blew her nose and wiped her face.

Millie was waiting for it. More lies.

Caprice stared at Sloane. The girl's brilliant blue eyes glistened. 'I . . .' she began. Millie was ready. 'I . . . I was feeling really homesick and Millie got homesick too.'

Millie flinched. She wondered what the girl was playing at.

'Don't worry. Everyone does sometimes,' Sloane said. But she wondered about Millie. That seemed strange.

Millie wanted to go back to her room but she didn't like the idea of leaving Caprice on her own with Sloane. She hovered on the other side of the table.

'I'm Sloane,' the girl said gently. 'You must be Caprice. We're sharing a room. Thanks for what you did before. It's never been like that in there – ever.'

Caprice nodded slowly. 'That's okay,' she snuffled.

'It probably won't stay that way for long,' Sloane said apologetically.

Caprice looked at her. 'I'm sure it will,' she said. There was an iciness to her voice that Millie didn't miss.

'You must be even more optimistic than Alice-Miranda,' Sloane grinned.

'No. I'm not.' Caprice shook her pretty head and pressed her lips tightly together.

The back door opened and Mrs Howard bustled through.

'Hello hello,' she greeted the three girls, failing to notice Millie's red face or Caprice's wet eyes. 'You're just the three I need. Mrs Smith has asked for some girls to help Charlie put out the extra tables and chairs in the dining room. Off you go.'

Millie opened her mouth to object when she saw Mrs Howard raise her eyebrow.

'Is something the matter, Millicent?'

Sloane answered for her. 'They were both just a bit homesick.'

Mrs Howard frowned. She'd never known Millie to be homesick in all the years she'd been at school. 'Really?'

Caprice gave a theatrical sniff. Millie nodded.

But Mrs Howard wasn't convinced. 'Well, in my experience there's nothing like some manual labour to take your mind off home.' She brushed her hands together. 'Off you go, girls. Charlie's in the dining room.'

'Don't worry,' Sloane said to Caprice as they headed out the door. 'You'll get used to it. I hated school when I first came but now I couldn't imagine being anywhere else.'

'Thanks.' Caprice smiled at the girl. 'It's good to have a friend.' She turned and narrowed her eyes at Millie, who thought she might be sick.

Chapter 5

Hugh Kennington-Jones scanned the page in his hand. He'd been going over the numbers for hours and the same solution kept bubbling to the surface. He was deep in thought when there was a knock at the study door.

Cecelia Highton-Smith popped her head around. 'Hello darling, can I interest you in a cup of tea and some chocolate cake? Dolly's been baking this morning and I have to say it's one of her best.'

'Ah, that would be lovely.' Hugh pushed the chair back and stood up, stretching his arms above his head. He turned and stared out the window across the field.

Cecelia set the tray down on the corner of the enormous leather-topped desk.

'Is something wrong, Hugh?' He had seemed preoccupied for the last few days.

Hugh spun around. 'I've been going through the finances for Pelham Park and I'm afraid the nursing home wing is costing far more than we ever expected. The apartments are fine, the residents purchase those and contribute to their upkeep, but we always said that we'd provide high care at no cost and I want to be able to keep doing that. It just has to be sustainable. I can't keep moving money from Kennington's to pay for it.'

Cecelia bit down on her pinkie nail. 'What are you thinking?'

'I don't know but the more I look at it the more I wonder if we're going to have to sell to one of those specialist aged-care providers,' Hugh replied.

'No, the whole model will change,' Cecelia said with alarm. 'We always said that we wanted the place to be about giving back. Half the residents are former staff of Highton's and Kennington's or people who've lived on the estates. I know Daisy has finally decided to book Granny Bert in too.'

'I know, I know. That's why I've been racking my brain.' Hugh poured the tea and then some milk into the fine china cup.

'Surely there must be something of value over there that we can sell. There's all that furniture and bric-a-brac in the cellar we said we'd send to auction one day.'

Hugh looked at his wife. A smile crept across his face. 'Oh, Cee, you're a genius!' He strode over and wrapped his arms around the woman and gave her a smacking great kiss on the lips.

'What was that for?' Cecelia giggled. 'I can't imagine that we'll make a fortune from a bunch of old sideboards and your father's predilection for stuffed animals.'

'No, not that.' Hugh shook his head. 'Mother's art collection. When she died, father had all of the paintings she loved taken down to the cellars and stored in a vault off to the side. He said he couldn't bear to look at it any more. I suspect that had as much to do with my brother's disappearance. I poked my head in there during the renovations and thought we should do something about it one of these days. But I hadn't given it another thought until now. Actually, it's unforgivable to have left it doing nothing all this time. It could be the answer to our problems.'

Cecelia frowned. 'I hadn't even realised there *was* a vault down there.' She had avoided the cellars during the transformation of the house, preferring to banish all those dreadful taxidermied beasts there. 'Is there much in the collection?'

'Masses. Mother loved her art and father hated it in equal measure, I think. I'm sure that some of it is museum- and gallery-worthy but we'll have to get someone in. I'm no authority.'

'Why don't you ask your brother to sort it out?' Cecelia suggested. 'He's always saying he wants to come and see us and this gives him a proper reason to be here. No more excuses that he's too busy – because this *is* work. Ed's an expert after all and he's family.'

'Do you think he'd come? There are so many bad memories for him at Pelham Park.' Hugh walked back to the desk and picked up his tea cup.

Ed Clifton was Hugh's elder brother by fourteen years. Hugh was just a small boy when he was told that his mother and brother had been killed in an accident, but that wasn't the truth at all. One fateful night, with the rain beating down and the thunder overhead, Hugh's brother had left home, defying his father's wish that he work in the family business. The young man, then known as Xavier, had decided to pursue his art. His mother had helped him leave and given him a painting, which she told him to sell to fund his studies.

The very next evening, Arabella Kennington-Jones was killed in a car accident. Hugh's father said that his brother was with her and he buried the two of them, side by side – except, of course, one of the coffins was empty.

Xavier set about building a new life for himself in New York. He donated the painting, a Renoir of a mother and her son, to the Metropolitan Museum, where he could look at it any time he liked and so could the rest of the world. He changed his name from Xavier to Edward, his middle name, which he paired with his mother's maiden name, Clifton. Over the years he became a highly successful artist and critic. He had long believed that his younger brother wasn't interested in a relationship with him, not knowing that Hugh had grown up thinking he'd died. It was only when Alice-Miranda visited New York with her parents that fate threw her together with her uncle, and the brothers were reunited.

'I was talking to him last week and mentioned the upcoming anniversary celebrations at Pelham Park. I said that he wouldn't know the place these days and he seemed interested. He was asking lots of questions. Coming back might give him some sense of closure with your father and mother,' Cecelia said.

'You're absolutely right, and there's no harm in asking. He can only say no,' Hugh said thoughtfully.

'Why don't you call him now and explain what we're trying to do. He should have a chance to see if there's anything he'd like for himself anyway,' Cecelia suggested.

Hugh smiled at his wife. 'How do you do that?'

'Do what?' she asked.

'Make me fall in love with you again every single day.' Hugh sat down and picked up the telephone.

'It's a gift, darling.' Cecelia winked then turned and walked out the door.

Chapter 6

Louella Derby had just sat down when the phone rang.

'Good afternoon, Winchesterfield-Downsfordvale Academy for Proper Young Ladies, this is Louella Derby speaking.'

There was a long pause as she listened to the caller. 'Yes, of course. I'm sure that she'd be very happy to talk with you right away, Ma'am,' Louella said. 'May I just put you on hold for a moment?'

The secretary pressed the 'hold' button and then hesitated before buzzing the intercom.

Miss Grimm's tired voice came through. 'Is it urgent, Mrs Derby?'

'I'm so sorry to bother you, Miss Grimm. I know you've had a hectic day but there's someone you'll want to speak to on the other line.'

'I doubt there is anyone on earth that I want to speak to at the moment, even the Queen herself. And if it's the builder telling me about another problem, hang up. I'll call him back tomorrow when I have the energy to deal with whatever disaster he's going to throw at me time this time. Now I must get –'

'No, no, please don't hang up. It's Her Majesty,' Mrs Derby said quickly.

'Queen Georgiana?' Miss Grimm was suddenly wide awake. 'Why didn't you tell me? I suppose you tried but I was too busy feeling sorry for myself. Did she say what she wants?'

'Not exactly, but she's heard about the delay with the new boarding house and has a proposal that could be a lifesaver for both of you.'

'Well, don't just sit there talking, Mrs Derby. Put her through and, for heaven's sake, don't cut her off. I haven't got her direct line and it takes hours to get through that lady-in-waiting of hers. What's her name?'

'Marmalade,' Louella Derby replied.

'Yes, Mrs Marmalade. That woman's more terrifying than a terrier in a room full of tabbies,' Miss Grimm replied, smiling at the image.

There was a long silence.

'Well, what are you waiting for?' Miss Grimm snapped.

'You actually,' a deeper voice replied.

Ophelia Grimm almost fell off her chair. 'I beg your pardon, Your Majesty. I hadn't realised my secretary had transferred the call.'

Ophelia took a deep breath and tried to calm herself. Although she'd met the Queen on several occasions and hosted her for tea in the study, she still couldn't get used to the idea that the monarch of their country was on the other end of the telephone.

'How may I help, Your Majesty?' she asked.

'I was wondering if I might pop around and see you,' said Queen Georgiana. 'I have something to discuss and it might be easier if I laid it all out in front of you.'

Ophelia nodded fiercely then realised she hadn't actually replied. 'Yes, of course, Ma'am. Any time that suits.'

'What about in ten minutes? I'm over at Chesterfield Downs for the night. We had some new horses arrive this afternoon and I thought I'd come and see how they were settling in.'

'Certainly,' said Miss Grimm.

'And don't make a fuss. I'd rather no one knows I'm there. I was supposed to have this sorted out months ago – I'll look a right twit if it goes ahead and I haven't had it trialled.'

Ophelia was intrigued. 'Yes, Your Majesty, I won't breathe a word. Might I suggest your driver parks in the front? I'll come and open the main doors. The girls never use that side of the building and they should all be in the house getting ready for tea when you arrive.'

'Splendid. If we can come to some sort of arrangement, I rather hope you can tell the girls the good news this evening,' Queen Georgiana said. 'There's no time to lose. Hang on a tick, dear.' There was a short silence while Queen Georgiana ran her eyes over the proposal in front of her.

Ophelia Grimm wasn't certain that she was still on the line when suddenly Her Majesty's voice boomed, 'Oh, for heaven's sake!'

'Is everything all right, Ma'am?'

'I've just realised I need some boys for this as well. Right. Well . . . Yes, that's it. Can you get onto Professor Winterbottom and have him meet us too? The old boy owes me a favour. I gave him a hot tip in the first at Ellingworth. The man made a small fortune, I believe.' And with that Queen Georgiana hung up the telephone.

Miss Grimm dialled the number for Fayle School. She glanced at her watch, hoping the Professor hadn't already gone to tea. She was about to give up when he answered. Ophelia raced through the Queen's request, noting the favour she had done him, and the Professor said that he'd be over in a flash. She looked around her study. There was a pile of enrolment papers on the desk and several stacks of books that Miss Reedy had suggested the girls could study this term, which she wanted to read for herself.

'Mrs Derby!' Ophelia called as she reefed open the double doors.

Louella leapt from her seat. 'What's the matter, Miss Grimm?'

'Quickly, come and help me tidy up. The Queen's coming.' She picked up the papers from her desk and dumped them into the secretary's outstretched arms.

'When, Miss Grimm?' she asked as she balanced the pile and took them to her own desk.

'About ten minutes,' Ophelia replied.

'Goodness, she's always given us more warning than that,' Mrs Derby called over her shoulder.

'Not this time. And you're not to tell a soul. Help me get this done and then you can go and stand guard at the front doors. Oh, and Professor Winterbottom's on his way too.'

'Yes, Miss Grimm.' Mrs Derby raced back into the headmistress's study and cleared away the cup and saucer on her desk.

Chapter 7

The chair in the centre of the teachers' table sat empty, awaiting the arrival of the headmistress. Miss Reedy had held off for as long as she could, but had relented and directed the children to the servery half an hour ago. It wasn't fair to keep them waiting any longer and Mrs Smith was worried about the pasta drying out and the sauce becoming gluggy.

It had taken longer than usual to get everyone through but at least the horrendous noise had died down once the girls and staff were busy eating.

Miss Reedy leaned closer to Mr Plumpton and said quietly, 'I can't believe she's not here. Tonight of all nights.'

The man frowned. 'Yes, I'd have thought she'd have some announcements to make.'

'I can do the announcements, Josiah. It's just not a good look with the new teachers and students. I'm sure many of them have heard rumours of the past situation, when we never saw her at all. She's been so wonderful of late. I do hope nothing's wrong.' Miss Reedy scanned the tables, keeping an especially close eye on the latest arrivals. She had an excellent vantage point as the teachers' table sat on a small podium overlooking the room.

'She's probably been held up by the builders,' Mr Plumpton said. 'That stable conversion has turned into a bit of a nightmare.'

'Yes, well, surely the girls and teachers should come first?' Miss Reedy raised her eyebrows.

'I know my girl comes first,' he whispered. Miss Reedy's cheeks flushed bright red.

Mr Plumpton moved his right hand and brushed it against her left. She started as if he'd jabbed her with an electric cattle prod.

Miss Reedy leapt to her feet and pointed. 'You! Little girl with the blonde plaits, what's your name?'

The small child looked up and swallowed hard. Her eyes were fixed on Miss Reedy like a deer caught in the headlights of a speeding truck.

'Yes, you,' Miss Reedy said.

'Essie,' the girl squeaked.

'Hmm. Essie, are you acquainted with the objects known as cutlery? You know, knives and forks?'

The child nodded. 'Of course, Miss Reedy.'

'Then might I suggest that you use them?' the teacher said sternly. She'd caught the child picking up a strand of spaghetti with her fingers.

Several other girls reached for their silverware.

Miss Reedy glared. Essie stared at her plate, not game to look up again. The teacher slowly sat down.

'Goodness me, what are the parents teaching these children? It's no wonder they ship them off to boarding school – at least we still have a focus on manners.' Miss Reedy shook her head and concentrated on her own meal.

Across the room, Caprice Radford twirled her fork around the long strands of pasta with an expert touch. She'd had a miraculous recovery from her alleged homesickness. 'Is she always so mean?'

Millie thought that was rich coming from Caprice.

'Oh no, Miss Reedy's not mean at all,' Alice-Miranda replied.

'But she is strict,' Sloane added. 'You don't want to get on her bad side.'

Jacinta looked up from where she was sitting opposite Caprice. 'We used to call her a fire-breathing dragon with a toothache. But she's not like that any more, not unless girls do something really awful.'

Caprice grinned. 'Sounds like a great name if you ask me. Who's that man next to her?'

'That's Mr Plumpton,' Alice-Miranda said. 'He's our Science teacher.'

Caprice snorted.

'What's so funny?' Alice-Miranda asked, wondering what the girl was getting at.

'Just look at him. He's the shape of a bowling pin and he's called "Plumpton" – seriously?' Caprice rolled her eyes.

'You're right.' Sloane giggled conspiratorially.

'Mr Plumpton's the sweetest man and you'll never meet anyone more passionate about their subject,' said Alice-Miranda. 'I think he's adorable.'

'How long's he been in love with the dragon lady?' asked Caprice, as she stared at the teachers.

'Oh, ages,' Sloane said.

Alice-Miranda really didn't like where this conversation was heading. 'So, what sport are you doing this term, Caprice?' she said loudly.

'Gymnastics,' the girl replied.

'Great,' said Jacinta. 'It will be good to have someone new on the team.' She'd hardly spoken to the girl, as Jacinta was among the year sevens who had to walk back from Caledonia Manor, but Sloane had told her about their room rescue on the way to dinner.

Millie's ears pricked up. 'Do you compete, Caprice?' It was the first time she'd spoken to her since the earlier incident.

'I've been school champion every year,' the girl replied.

Millie took a deep breath. Of course she was. 'Sounds like you might have yourself some proper competition, Jacinta,' Millie said.

Jacinta frowned.

'Why? Are you the school champion?' Caprice asked.

'She's the national champion,' Alice-Miranda said proudly. 'We hope we're going to be cheering her on at the Olympics one day.'

'So long as I stop injuring myself,' Jacinta said with a shrug.

Caprice gulped. Millie was enjoying watching the girl squirm.

'Actually, I think I picked tennis for this term,' Caprice said, biting her lip.

Millie eyeballed the girl. 'Really? Great. That's my thing.'

'Millie's amazing,' Alice-Miranda said.

'Are you the national champion too?' Caprice asked tartly.

Millie shook her head. 'No, but I'm looking forward to playing against you.'

Miss Reedy stood up and walked to the microphone at the end of the teacher's table. 'Girls, we'll start lining up for dessert. It looks like Mrs Smith has outdone herself with –' she squinted – 'is that apple pie and ice-cream?'

Doreen Smith gave a decisive nod from behind the servery.

'Well done! And in difficult circumstances, might I add. Now, we'll do this in an orderly fashion and I'd ask you to keep the noise down, please. It was quite unbearable earlier and I won't put up with that again.'

Miss Reedy pointed at the table in front of her. 'Off you go, girls.'

Chairs scraped across the floorboards as the children stood up, clattering cutlery and plates. Just as the group was about to move off, a pair of high heels clack-clacked across the floorboards.

'Hello everyone, I'm so sorry I'm late,' Miss Grimm apologised loudly as she strode to the podium at the far end of the room. Her red suit stood out like a beacon and her smile was positively beaming. Alice-Miranda thought she looked as lovely as ever.

Miss Reedy looked at the girls in front of her and indicated that they should sit back down.

A hush fell over the room.

Miss Reedy stepped back from the microphone. Ophelia Grimm smoothed her hair and clasped her hands in front of her before she began to speak.

'Good evening, girls, staff. I am terribly sorry for being late. Mr Grump sends his regards too. Poor man has a cold and he was eager not to share his germs. I'm sure that you're going to find what I'm about to tell you very exciting. As you're all well aware, we've had some delays with the new boarding house. Things are rather uncomfortable for everyone at Grimthorpe House and in here too.' She peered across the room. 'You look like marbles in a jar out there. But I have an announcement that will solve all our problems.'

The teachers stared at one another in puzzlement.

'What's going on?' Benitha Wall, the PE teacher, said to Mr Trout. She spoke far louder than she'd meant to.

'If you'd be so kind as to wait a second, Miss Wall, I'll tell you.' Ophelia Grimm scowled at the woman, who slumped down in her chair, trying to make herself invisible – which was quite difficult, considering she was over six feet tall and almost half as wide.

'Professor Winterbottom and I have been tasked with trialling a new and exciting award scheme for none other than –' She paused for a moment – 'Queen Georgiana herself. The program is aimed at students from the ages of eight to fourteen, so that includes all current Winchesterfield-Downsfordvale students. We don't have anyone under eight at the moment.' Miss Grimm winked at Alice-Miranda, who smiled back. 'The award requires the demonstration of resilience, respect, self-discipline, courage, creativity and service to the community. Under normal circumstances we'd be able to complete the activities over a slightly longer period. However, as we are trialling the program, which is due to be rolled out across the country before the end of term, Queen Georgiana has asked that we get cracking right away. The overall award will be known as the Queen's Colours but you will be working towards the first level, the Queen's Blue. I do hope that all of you will be capable of achieving it. I'm also very excited that there will be a special award for the student who achieves the highest individual point score. Over the years to come, you will be able to complete further levels towards the ultimate prize of the Queen's Colours, which will be awarded at a ceremony at the palace. That, however, is still a way off yet.'

A murmur shot around the room as the girls and teachers began to speculate.

'Quiet, everyone,' Miss Grimm ordered. 'Tomorrow afternoon, all one hundred and twenty-five of you and the teachers will be heading off to camp.'

A huge cheer went up around the room. Some girls hugged their neighbours and others jumped up and down in their seats.

A self-satisfied look crept onto Caprice's face. That special award was hers.

'Camp? Is she joking?' Mr Trout asked.

'No, I'm certainly not joking, Mr Trout.' Miss Grimm smiled at the man. 'And this is not just any old camp. This is camp, community service, physical challenges, time for the choir to shine and a dozen other things all rolled into one.'

Mrs Smith wiped her brow with the back of her hand. 'What a blessed relief,' she whispered.

Miss Reedy took a step forward and whispered in the headmistress's ear. 'But Miss Grimm, Miss Wall and I have spent hours arranging the camp for just before the half-term break. We can't possibly rearrange things at such short notice. Do you have any idea how hard it is to get a last-minute camp site booking?'

Ophelia Grimm turned to the English teacher. 'Miss Reedy, as one of the finest staff members in this school, surely you remember that the first rule of being a good educator is flexibility. Her Majesty has offered us this opportunity and, given that we have a number of problems with the facilities at the moment, I have taken it with both hands. There is a program written for the entire duration of the camp and I'm sure that you will find the amenities surprisingly comfortable in your role as camp coordinator.'

'Me?' Miss Reedy asked, scowling.

'Yes, Miss Reedy, we've decided that you and Mr Lipp will be in charge of the camp. Professor Winterbottom must stay at Fayle to look after the boys who are not attending and I have to stay here to make sure that all of the building and maintenance is finished by the time you return.'

'But, but,' Miss Reedy protested. 'That's huge. How many boys are coming? And really – Mr Lipp? Again?'

'But nothing, Miss Reedy. It's time to rise to the occasion and show me how you can shine. The Winchester-Fayle Singers will have an event at the end of camp, so I expect them to be primed to do their best as always. We need Mr Lipp to attend to their rehearsals. And in answer to your question, there will be a relatively small number of boys attending. Just the singers and a few extras.'

Beads of perspiration were dotted along Mr Plumpton's brow. He couldn't believe that he'd have to deal with Harry Lipp again so soon. The man was incorrigible, as he had proved during their trip to Paris where he did his best to woo Miss Reedy.

Miss Reedy gulped. 'When are we leaving?' she asked quietly.

'The destination is sorted and Mrs Derby has been on the telephone arranging buses so, all things being equal, you must be ready to go tomorrow at midday. You'll be back again on Saturday,' Miss Grimm explained.

Miss Reedy did the calculations in her head. 'I suppose five days is bearable,' she said. 'Just.'

Miss Grimm stepped back up to the microphone. 'Now, girls, the only thing you need to do is collect a packing list from Mrs Derby on your way out and organise your bag as soon as you get to the house. Teachers, I'll need you all to remain behind so we can go through the arrangements.'

Chapter 8

Somehow, in less than twenty-four hours, bags had been packed, parents informed and now the girls were waiting to board their transport to camp. A fleet of buses lined the driveway outside Winchesterfield Manor. The campers were still completely unaware of their destination, as Miss Grimm had decided it was more fun to leave things as a surprise.

'Right.' Miss Reedy stalked along the path armed with a clipboard and a whistle. She was dressed in khaki trousers and a white shirt with hiking boots and a straw hat. 'Alice-Miranda, Millie, Caprice, Sloane and Jacinta, you're on the last bus. Take your things. Off you go.'

'What about the boys?' Jacinta asked the teacher. 'Are they coming on the same buses as us?'

'You just want to see your boyfriend,' Sloane teased.

'I do not,' Jacinta retorted, but of course that was exactly what she had in mind. Except that Jacinta wasn't even sure that Lucas was attending the camp. Things had happened so quickly she hadn't been able to find out anything.

'How come we're on a minibus when everyone else has a coach?' Caprice grumbled as the girls made their way to the last vehicle in the line.

She hadn't heard Miss Reedy's footsteps behind them.

'Just lucky I guess, Caprice. Given the swiftness of the arrangements you're fortunate not to be walking,' the teacher quipped.

'Oh, you misunderstood me, Miss Reedy. I love minibuses,' the child said sweetly.

'I am sorry, Caprice. I've heard a lot of whining this morning,' the teacher apologised.

'That's all right, Miss Reedy. Is there anything I can do to help?' Caprice asked.

'No, everything's under control but thank you so much for asking.' Miss Reedy walked away to check on the other girls.

Millie couldn't believe the cheek of the girl.

The group hopped on board and were surprised to find Mr Plumpton in the driver's seat.

'Good afternoon, ladies,' he said cheerily. 'Welcome aboard the Plumpton Express.'

Alice-Miranda grinned. 'Hello Mr Plumpton. I didn't realise you could drive a minibus.'

'It's not often my skills are called upon but today there was no alternative. Charlie's taken the school bus to be fixed, and Mrs Derby could only get three coaches at such short notice, so it was fortunate I could take the wheel.' He noticed the new student and nodded at her. 'You must be Caprice. My name's Mr Plumpton. I'll be teaching your science lessons, when I'm not driving a bus.'

Millie was keen to hear Caprice's response, after the girl had mocked the man so horribly at dinner the night before.

'I love science,' Caprice said warmly. 'I was reading *Scientific American* last month. Did you see that article about the Higgs boson?

'Oh yes, fascinating,' Mr Plumpton replied, clearly enchanted by the girl.

'I'm sure that it will change the world of physics,' Caprice said.

'Do you often read about science?' Mr Plumpton asked.

'Mmm, sometimes. I like medical journals too.'

Millie rolled her eyes.

Mr Plumpton's grin grew wider. Apart from Alice-Miranda he didn't really have any students he considered prodigies. Perhaps that was about to change.

The girls sat down, Millie and Alice-Miranda on one side and Jacinta and Sloane on the other. Caprice sat on her own in front of the older girls.

Millie leaned forward and called out to Mr Plumpton, 'Who else is coming with us?'

Just as she did, Miss Reedy hopped on board. 'Only the five of you,' she said.

'A whole minibus for us?' Sloane said. 'Couldn't we have just taken a couple of cars instead?'

'We could have but then we wouldn't fit the Fayle boys and Mr Lipp in, would we?' Miss Reedy replied. 'Buckle up, girls.'

Jacinta's face exploded into a grin.

'Look at you!' Sloane laughed.

'What?' Jacinta tried to stop smiling. 'Well, I haven't seen Lucas for weeks and we're just good friends, that's all.'

'For now maybe,' Sloane said.

Jacinta nodded. 'Until we're old enough to get married.'

Caprice looked over her shoulder at the pair. 'Is he cute?'

'He's gorgeous,' Jacinta replied.

Sloane whispered, '*And* his father's a movie star.'

'Oh really?' Caprice sounded dubious. 'Who is he?'

'Lawrence Ridley,' Sloane said casually.

'I've met him,' Caprice replied. 'He came to one of Mummy's parties.'

Millie was listening from the other side of the aisle. As if, she thought to herself, but kept quiet.

'Does Lucas look like his father?' Caprice asked.

'Yes,' Jacinta replied.

'Maybe I'll save him a seat.' Caprice grinned like a fox and turned back to the front.

Jacinta's forehead wrinkled. 'Did you hear that?' she whispered to Sloane. 'You have to move. Go and sit next to her.'

Sloane shook her head. 'Why?'

'Are you kidding? Haven't you noticed how pretty she is? No, not pretty. She's perfect.'

Caprice looked back around. 'Do you think I can't hear you? And don't worry, Jacinta, I have no interest in stealing your little boyfriend. I'm sure that Lucas has a mind of his own.' She smiled her megawatt smile.

Jacinta didn't know whether to be relieved or not.

Soon the little diesel bus clattered into the driveway at the Fayle School. About twenty boys were standing on the path, laden with backpacks and sleeping bags. Mr Lipp was wearing a beige safari suit and marching about barking orders at the boys.

'Who's that?' Caprice snorted. 'And seriously, what is he wearing?'

'That's Mr Lipp,' Alice-Miranda said. 'He's a fashionista.'

'That's one word for him,' Sloane said. 'Let's just say that he doesn't like to blend in.'

The boys loaded their bags into the small boot at the back of the bus then clambered on board with their day packs.

'Back seat's mine,' George 'Figgy' Figworth yelled as he charged down the aisle.

‘Hello George,’ Alice-Miranda called as he sped past.

George grinned. ‘Morning, pipsqueak. Didn’t realise we were sharing the bus with you girls.’

Rufus Pemberley followed his friend and the two lads stretched out across the back seat.

‘What a lovely surprise, little sister.’ Sep Sykes’s voice dripped with sarcasm as he and Lucas walked past the girls and slid into the seats behind them.

‘Don’t blame me,’ said Sloane, rolling her eyes. ‘I’d rather not see you either.’

The twenty Fayle boys quickly filled the spare seats. Miss Reedy sat behind Mr Plumpton and Mr Lipp was directly across the aisle.

‘Well, this is an unexpected pleasure,’ Harold Lipp told Miss Reedy.

From his spot in the driver’s seat, Mr Plumpton was on high alert. Harry Lipp had no shame. But in the end it was he who had taken Livinia out in Paris and it was Josiah Plumpton who had continued to court her over the term break. Their romance was still under wraps for now. Alice-Miranda was the only one who knew and she was a most trustworthy child.

‘I’m sorry, Mr Lipp, but what are you talking about?’ Miss Reedy asked stiffly.

‘This. An expedition and so early in the term. We were stunned when the Professor gave the go ahead. I mean, we’d only been at school a day and the old boy’s usually so strict about outings in the first month. Queen Georgiana must have promised the Professor something fairly impressive to get him to agree.’

‘Oh, I’m sure she can be very persuasive,’ Miss Reedy replied.

‘Have you read all this bumf about the camp?’ Mr Lipp asked, holding up his folder.

‘Yes, of course.’ Miss Reedy nodded. ‘Have you?’

‘All this?’ He scoffed and waved it in the air. ‘I only received it last night. You can fill me in on the way.’

‘I think you’d better read it for yourself, Mr Lipp,’ Miss Reedy said tartly.

‘But I’ll be sick. I couldn’t possibly.’ Harry pouted and did his best impression of puppy-dog eyes.

‘Oh, for heaven’s sake. In the interests of making sure that we do everything properly, I’ll tell you,’ said Miss Reedy. She gave him a withering look.

Chapter 9

Hugh Kennington-Jones pulled up outside the arrivals hall and manoeuvred the silver Range Rover into the kerb. An endless stream of vehicles came and went every few seconds.

Cecelia scanned the throng of people spilling out of the building.

'There he is, darling.' She opened the car door and scurried across the pavement. 'Ed! Over here!'

A tall, well-dressed man with a thick crop of

salt-and-pepper hair strode out of the airport, pulling a black bag behind him.

'Cecelia!' Ed enveloped her in a warm embrace.

'It's wonderful to see you. We're so excited that you agreed to come,' Cecelia enthused. 'The car's just over here.'

Hugh left the vehicle idling, hopped out and opened the tailgate.

'Hello little brother.' Ed reached out to shake Hugh's hand.

'It's so good to have you here,' said Hugh. His eyes twinkled. A year ago he never thought he'd be welcoming his big brother home again.

'How's that gorgeous little niece of mine?' Ed asked as he climbed into the back seat.

'She's great. Just started back at school but oddly enough is off to camp today,' Hugh said.

'That's a bit soon, isn't it?' Ed said. 'Not that I remember much about school these days.'

Hugh glanced at him in the rear-vision mirror. 'Apparently Aunty Gee had something to do with it. The school is doing her a huge favour and things are in a bit of a mess at Winchesterfield-Downsfordvale with some late-running renovations, so it's worked out well for everyone. And what's even better is that the kids are going to Bagley Hall and spending some of their time doing service activities at Pelham Park.'

Ed frowned. 'Back up a moment, little brother. Who's Aunty Gee?'

'Sorry, Ed. There are so many things I assume you know but of course you don't. Aunty Gee is otherwise known as Queen Georgiana and she's um . . .'

'She's Mummy's best friend and my and Charlotte's godmother,' Cecelia finished for him.

'Wow. That's intimidating,' Ed said with a grin.

'Not at all, darling. Wait until you meet her. She's a hoot and far more down-to-earth than the press makes her out to be,' Cecelia explained. 'Mummy's much more terrifying.'

'Second question. Bagley Hall? Do you mean the enormous old manor next to Pelham Park, where that ogre Mrs Marchant used to live when we were kids?'

Hugh nodded. 'One and the same.'

'I thought she was about a hundred when I was a boy. Gosh, she must have seemed like she'd stepped off the Ark to you,' Ed said.

Hugh nodded. 'She scared the socks off me. When the old bird died her family struggled to keep the place afloat. Her grand-nephew was teaching PE at one of the local schools and hit on the idea of turning the property into a kids' camp. The camp's been open for about ten years now and it's amazing – won all sorts of awards and has Aunty Gee's royal warrant.'

'Things have changed, haven't they?' Ed said with a smile. Of course, he thought, it was inevitable after being away for almost forty years.

Cecelia turned around in her seat. 'We're going home to Highton Hall tonight. I know Mrs Oliver has been baking up a storm and Shilly has the house sparkling from top to bottom. Then tomorrow we'll drive up to Pelham Park so you can assess exactly how big this job will be.'

'Great.' Ed nodded. 'I wish I could remember more of what Mother had but I'm afraid it's a bit of a blur. It will be strange to be there again.'

'Well, let's just hope that you find the place a lot less foreboding than I did when I was young. We made Dad's den into a games room for the oldies, so there are no dead bears or other wildlife on the walls any more. Cee did a great job of brightening the place up. It's quite lovely and the gardens have given the house new life. The old man must be turning in his grave with those masses of flowerbeds everywhere.'

The trio drove along in silence for a few minutes.

'Was he awful to you, Hugh?' Ed asked quietly.

Hugh Kennington-Jones caught his brother's eye in the rear-view mirror. 'He never lost his edges, but I suppose we got along because I fell in love with the grocery business, and he was happy to have someone continue the family legacy. I can't agree with everything he did, but I think he was just about the loneliest man alive much of the time. I wonder if he ever had a proper friend.'

Ed nodded. 'I was angry with him, but as I grew older I felt sad for him too, actually. I got to live my dreams, but I'm not convinced that he did. I guess we'll never know. Anyway, enough of that melancholy. Tell me about Highton Hall.'

A smile spread across Cecelia's face. Hugh caught it. 'Oh no, Ed, you do realise that Cee won't stop talking between now and home. You'll know the names, birthdates and preferred underpants colour of every single person who lives on the estate,' Hugh teased.

'Don't be ridiculous, darling.' Cecelia gave him a playful poke in the ribs. 'Although I did see that Granny Bert had some of the most enormous knickers hanging on the line at the back of Rose Cottage. I wondered if she'd taken up parachuting.'

Hugh and Ed laughed.

Chapter 10

Alice-Miranda and Millie were playing a game of 'I Spy' as the little bus chugged along to their mystery camp site.

'I can't believe Miss Grimm hasn't told us where we're going,' Millie said. She was peering around the bus and out the windows, trying to guess what Alice-Miranda was thinking of that started with the letter 'I'.

'It's good to have a surprise,' Alice-Miranda said and shrugged.

'What if the camp is horrible? We don't even know if we have to sleep in tents or if there are dormitories or how many of us will have to share. It might be an old barn in the middle of nowhere, with outside toilets. Gross!' Millie griped.

'What do you have against outside toilets? You have to go all the way across the caravan park to the toilets when you're at the beach,' Alice-Miranda replied.

'Mmm, true,' Millie conceded.

From the back of the bus there was a loud thud followed by peals of laughter.

Miss Reedy turned around to see George Figworth sitting on the floor, having been wrestled out of his seat by Rufus Pemberley.

'What on earth are you two doing? Get back into your seat and put your seatbelt on immediately, Figworth, or you can spend the rest of the journey up here beside me. Is that what you'd prefer?' she asked menacingly.

Figgy scrambled back onto the seat and yanked at the seatbelt.

'Is it an idiot?' Millie said.

Alice-Miranda frowned. 'What are you talking about?'

'I Spy. Is it those two idiots?' She gestured towards the back of the bus.

Alice-Miranda laughed and shook her head. 'No, it's not them.'

'I give up then,' Millie said.

'It's interior lights,' Caprice piped up from the other side of the aisle.

'Yes, you've got it.' Alice-Miranda clapped her hands together. 'I thought that was a tricky one. Well done.'

'No, it wasn't,' Caprice scoffed. 'I can think of much harder things than that.'

'Well, it's your turn now,' Alice-Miranda said.

'"S".' Caprice turned back to the front of the bus, a smug smile plastered on her face.

Millie looked around. 'Is it seats?'

'No.'

Sloane weighed in. 'Seatbelts?'

'Wrong,' Caprice said. 'You'll never get it.'

'What about sun visor?' Alice-Miranda said thoughtfully.

Caprice sighed loudly, her shoulders slumping.

'Ha! She's right, isn't she?' Millie said.

'No!' Caprice shook her head. 'That wasn't it at all.'

'You're lying, Caprice,' Millie said. 'It was sun visor and now you're just saying it wasn't because you don't think anyone is as clever as you.'

Alice-Miranda touched Millie's arm. 'It's okay, Millie. If it wasn't, I'm fine with that. We can keep playing.'

Jacinta called out 'sun roof'. Then she looked up and realised the bus didn't actually have one.

'The game's finished,' Caprice announced. She picked up the magazine that was sitting on the empty seat beside her.

'Of course it is. Because Alice-Miranda guessed. You know what, Caprice? People around here like to play fair,' Millie chided.

Sloane looked across the aisle and raised her eyebrows at Millie.

'I do play fair.' Caprice turned and wrinkled her nose at Millie. 'You don't know anything about me.'

'Oh, yes I do. You might be able to fool everyone else but you don't fool me. For a start, you *think* you know everything,' Millie snapped.

'Well, I know a lot more than you,' Caprice bit back.

Miss Reedy peered around to check that Figgy was back in his seat and noticed Millie leaning out into the aisle. The girl's face was bright red and she seemed to be sputtering words all over the place.

'What's wrong with you? You're such a fake!' Millie huffed.

'It's okay, Millie. Calm down,' Alice-Miranda soothed. Millie had told Alice-Miranda what she'd heard Caprice saying about her the afternoon before. But when Alice-Miranda said that she'd speak to the girl, Millie begged her not to. She was sure that Caprice would deny everything.

Miss Reedy unclasped her seatbelt and stood up. She walked down the centre of the bus, eyeballing Millie and Caprice in turn. 'Is everything all right?'

'Fine,' Millie lied.

'No,' Caprice sniffed. 'She's being mean to me!' Tears began to flood the girl's cheeks. Within seconds her sobs turned into great big hiccupy gulps. 'I want to go home,' Caprice wailed.

'Millie, what happened?' Miss Reedy fished around in her pocket and produced a tissue, which she held out to Caprice.

'Nothing. I wasn't mean to her. She cheated in the game.' Millie could feel her eyes prickling but she was determined not to cry.

'Perhaps you should apologise, Millie,' Miss Reedy suggested.

'Why? I didn't do anything. She's faking it! They're crocodile tears,' Millie blurted.

By now Mr Lipp was aware of the sobbing and had stood up to join Miss Reedy.

'Oh, dear me, whatever's the matter?' the teacher asked Caprice.

The girl let out several short gasps as another torrent of tears trickled down her cheeks.

'This is Caprice,' Miss Reedy explained. 'She's new and I think she and Millie might have had a difference of opinion.'

Millie crossed her arms in front of her and stared at the ground.

'Caprice?' Mr Lipp enquired. 'You're the new girl Mr Trout telephoned me about last night. The one with the voice.'

Caprice looked up through a haze of tears and nodded slowly.

'My dear, we can't have this, can we? Why don't you come and sit at the front with Miss Reedy and me and you can tell us all about it. Then, when you're feeling better, we can talk about a song I've been thinking the group should try. We haven't had a strong enough soloist for it yet but Mr Trout told me that was all about to change,' Mr Lipp gushed.

Sloane and Jacinta looked at each other from their seat behind Caprice, their mouths flapping open. Up until now they had been taking turns for most of the solo parts in the Winchester-Fayle Singers and as far as they knew, Mr Lipp had been very happy with their efforts. This was news to them.

'What about us?' Sloane demanded.

'Oh, Sloane, Jacinta, you're both wonderful, of course, but this part requires a voice with that little bit extra,' Mr Lipp blustered.

'But you haven't even heard her sing!' Jacinta complained.

'I don't need to. I trust Mr Trout's judgement, and he said that she's the most naturally gifted vocalist he's ever encountered in all his years of teaching. You heard her too, didn't you Miss Reedy?' Mr Lipp queried.

The woman nodded.

'And?'

'Caprice has a lovely voice.' Miss Reedy didn't want to talk Caprice up too much at that moment. She was patently aware of how annoyed Sloane and Jacinta were already.

'I've heard that lovely isn't the half of it,' Mr Lipp replied. 'Come along, Caprice. Shall we have a chat?'

Mr Lipp waited for the girl to stand and then ushered her to the front seat. Miss Reedy decided there was no point pursuing the incident until she had a chance to speak with Millie on her own, so she followed them back to her seat.

Millie watched them go. As Caprice turned to sit down, her lip curled and she grinned like a Cheshire cat.

'Oh!' Millie gasped. 'Did you see that?'

But Jacinta and Sloane were too busy sniping about losing their solos and Alice-Miranda was looking out the window.

Alice-Miranda reached out and patted her friend on the arm. 'I'll talk to her when we get to camp. Try not to let her get to you.'

But it was much too late for that. Caprice had crawled right under Millie's skin and she wasn't going anywhere.

Chapter 11

Josiah Plumpton leaned closer to the steering wheel. His right foot pressed hard against the accelerator pedal but it had no effect on the little white bus's speed. Its diesel engine clattered loudly as it chugged to the top of the hill. *I think I can, I think I can.* The teacher smiled to himself as the childish words repeated in his head.

Livinia Reedy was sitting directly behind him and organising the children into their camp groups. Ideally she would have had it all done before they'd left, but even with a couple of hours off class that morning there still hadn't been enough time. She was beginning to rethink where to put Caprice too – obviously she and Millie weren't a good combination but Alice-Miranda would be a positive influence. Across the aisle, Harold Lipp was interrogating Caprice about her singing experience.

'Mr Trout told me that you won the National Eisteddfod last year,' he gushed.

Caprice sniffed and nodded.

Miss Reedy thought the girl looked remarkably unblemished for someone who had spent the past twenty minutes crying.

'We're going to have choir practice this evening,' said Mr Lipp. 'I'm looking forward to hearing you sing.'

Caprice stared up at him, her blue eyes shining. 'I could sing for you now.'

'Oh no, you've been upset. Your voice might not be at its best. That wouldn't be fair at all.'

Caprice blinked away the last of her tears and shrugged. 'I don't mind.'

Livinia Reedy interrupted. 'Perhaps not now, Caprice. You wouldn't want the other children to think that you were showing off, would you?'

'But Mr Lipp said that he'd like to hear me,' the girl retorted. Then, ignoring Miss Reedy's suggestion, she cleared her throat and began.

At first she sang softly. No one further back could hear her but as she reached the chorus she raised the volume and the chatter on the bus stopped.

'Hey Mr Plumpton,' Figgy called out. 'Can you turn the radio up? We can't hear it properly down the back.'

'That's not the radio,' said Alice-Miranda, her brown eyes widening.

Millie sighed. 'No, it's Little Miss Perfect.'

'Wow! She's amazing . . .' The boys were all talking over the top of one another and nodding in agreement.

Sloane and Jacinta looked at each other. 'There go our solos,' said Sloane.

Caprice's high note warbled for what seemed like an age before she stopped and Figgy let out a whoop and a cheer that got the whole bus going.

Caprice smiled at Mr Lipp, whose grin almost touched each ear.

'Mr Trout was absolutely right,' he gushed. 'Your voice is the nearest thing to perfection I've ever heard.'

'Encore, encore,' Figgy yelled from the back seat.

'I think that's probably enough for now,' Miss Reedy said, and pursed her lips.

Caprice was about to say otherwise when Figgy called out again. 'Hey Mr Plumpton, there's a police car behind us.'

Miss Reedy turned around in her seat. 'George Figworth, please keep your voice down. I'm quite sure that Mr Plumpton is well aware of what's going on behind him.'

'Have you been speeding, sir?' the boy shouted.

'Figworth!' The English teacher gave the lad her best evil stare. He opened his mouth like a fish then closed it again.

'As if.' Rufus Pemberley laughed. 'We could walk faster than this old bomb.'

Mr Plumpton glanced in the rear-vision mirror again. He'd first noticed the police car a few miles back when it had sped up behind them. The officer had pulled out to overtake but slipped back into the left lane and stayed there. Josiah wondered if there was a problem, but he couldn't imagine for a second what it was. Unless a tail-light was out. The bus had been hired from Downsfordvale, as Charlie had taken the school bus to be repaired. Rufus was right when he said that they couldn't have been speeding. It simply wasn't possible.

Josiah spotted the exit to Dunleavy and put on his indicator. The police car followed.

'It's still there,' Figgy updated the passengers.

By now several more of the children were trying to guess why they were being followed. Everyone had forgotten about Caprice's impromptu performance.

'I know where we are,' said Alice-Miranda, as she looked out the window at the pretty countryside. 'Pelham Park is just up the road. That's where Daddy grew up. He and Mummy have turned it into an aged-care home. And there's an amazing camp next door called Bagley Hall. It's got the most incredible facilities. There's a ropes course and a climbing wall, canoeing, cycling, archery – just about everything, I think.'

'Cool!' Millie started to sound like her usual self again. 'I hope we're going there.'

Alice-Miranda grinned. 'Me too.'

'Whoa, that's a mansion and a half,' exclaimed Sep Sykes. He didn't know it but he was admiring Pelham Park, which sat atop a rise well back from the road and down a tree-lined driveway.

‘This is it,’ Mr Plumpton called as the bus came to a halt. He was waiting for the traffic to pass so he could turn right.

Suddenly the police car’s siren blared.

‘Hey Mr Plumpton, you’d better pull over,’ Rufus Pemberley shouted. ‘Looks like you’re in trouble.’

The children laughed.

The teacher ignored the lad’s taunts.

‘What’s going on, Josiah?’ Miss Reedy craned her neck to see the car behind them.

‘I don’t know. I haven’t done anything wrong.’

Mr Lipp was twitching in his seat. ‘Well, you’d better pull over. I don’t like this at all.’

‘I can’t stop here. This road’s too dangerous. I’ll just pull into the driveway.’ Josiah saw a gap in the traffic and planted his foot on the accelerator much harder than he’d meant to. The bus wheels spun and the vehicle lurched forward, jolting the children from side to side.

‘Are you gonna outrun him, sir?’ Figgy yelled. Several of the boys roared with laughter.

As the bus flew through the gates the police car sped past and skidded to a halt in front of it.

Mr Plumpton stomped on the brake and his

passengers were thrown forward. Fortunately they were held in by their seatbelts.

'Steady on there, Plumpy! You'll kill us all!' Mr Lipp exploded as his head stopped just short of hitting the metal bar in front of him.

A tall thin woman wearing navy trousers and a white shirt stepped out of the police car. She rapped sharply on the driver's window and demanded that Mr Plumpton open the door.

'What did you do, sir?' Rufus Pemberley called. The children leapt up from their seats to see what was happening.

'Sit down, everyone,' Miss Reedy barked from the front of the vehicle. 'Don't move a muscle – or else.'

The children reluctantly returned to their seats.

Mr Plumpton pulled the lever and the bus door opened with a whoosh.

The woman held up a shiny silver badge as she walked up the stairs and onto the bus.

'Can you see what's going on?' Alice-Miranda asked as Millie craned her neck to try to get a better look at the officer.

'I'm DS Freeman. You, you and you.' She pointed at the three teachers. 'Off the bus, please.'

For the first time on the journey, you could have heard a pin drop.

'I beg your pardon.' Mr Lipp stood up. 'What on earth's going on? We could have been killed the way you pulled in front of us like a maniac.'

DS Freeman pursed her lips. 'You look fine to me.'

'Well, what has Plumpton done wrong?' Mr Lipp demanded. Tiny beads of perspiration sprang up along his moustache like dewdrops on a spring lawn.

'Is this your vehicle?' the policewoman asked Mr Plumpton.

'No,' he replied.

'That's all I needed to know. I am arresting you for being in possession of a stolen vehicle.'

Mr Plumpton gasped. 'Stolen?'

'Yes, you heard me.'

'Stolen!' Rufus blurted. 'Cool!'

'Yeah, and they kidnapped us too,' Figgy yelled, waving his hands in the air. 'And they're holding us against our will. We're just a bunch of innocent kids. Please help us.'

'Stop it, Figworth,' Miss Reedy barked.

DS Freeman looked up at the children. It was as if she hadn't registered their presence at all until that moment. 'What are they doing here?' she asked, a look of uncertainty creeping across her face.

'There must be a mistake, detective sergeant,' Mr Plumpton said softly. 'You see, we're on a school trip. I hired the bus this morning.'

'I can assure you I've checked, and you are driving stolen property,' the woman said firmly. 'Would you step outside, please?'

Mr Plumpton and Miss Reedy hopped off the bus, followed by Mr Lipp.

The officer took one last look at the children.

Alice-Miranda shuffled past Millie and scurried towards the front of the bus. 'Excuse me,' she said as the woman was about to depart. 'My name is Alice-Miranda Highton-Smith-Kennington-Jones and I'm very pleased to meet you. Mr Lipp was telling you the truth. We are on a school trip. In fact, we're on a school trip because Queen Georgiana arranged it for us. George was just joking about us being kidnapped. He's like that, always playing tricks.' She glanced around at the boy, who had a smirk on his face. Some of the other children were looking daggers at the lad.

DS Freeman gulped. 'Queen Georgiana, you say?'

Alice-Miranda nodded.

The detective sergeant couldn't imagine why the Queen would send children to camp in a stolen vehicle. 'Stay right there.' She hopped off the bus and joined the teachers outside. She had a bad feeling about this.

Alice-Miranda followed her to the door.

The children on the right side of the bus rushed into the aisle, eager to see what was happening.

Mr Lipp's arms were flying wildly in the air, just as they did when he was conducting, and Miss Reedy's face was set in a scowl. Mr Plumpton cupped his hands to his cherry-red cheeks. Detective Sergeant Freeman wore a heavy frown.

'I wonder what they're saying,' said Jacinta.

'Look!' Millie gasped.

The detective sergeant produced a shiny pair of handcuffs and held them up at Mr Plumpton.

Figgy wrestled with one of the bus windows and slid it open so the children could hear what was going on.

'This is an outrage!' Mr Lipp was sputtering and spluttering. 'You can't be serious about arresting Mr Plumpton. I demand to speak to your superior.'

'Plumpy's being arrested!' Figgy turned to the children and called out in horror. The boy barged his way to the front of the bus and leapt off. 'No, no! I didn't mean it. We're not kidnapped. It was just a joke!'

'Get back on that bus,' the detective sergeant fumed.

'But I . . . I just said that to be funny,' Figgy pleaded.

She glowered at the boy. 'Well, you're not.'

'Look, this is ridiculous,' said Miss Reedy. The teacher was shaking. 'Call the hire company.'

DS Freeman glanced back at the bus and the children sitting with their mouths open like a bowl of gasping goldfish. 'All right, stay there.' She glared at the three teachers and the boy with his mop of wild hair.

Back in the police car, Fenella Freeman radioed through to the station.

'Wilson, where are you?' she barked into the handpiece.

There was a crackle and an explosion of static.

'Yes, DS,' came the reply.

'Where have you been? Oh, never mind. I need you to look up a registration for me.' She spat out the sequence of letters and numbers. 'Check the status of that vehicle, will you?'

'It's a white minibus, listed as stolen from Downsfordvale,' Constable Wilson replied.

'Good, thanks, that's all I needed to know. I've just located it.' Fenella smiled smugly to herself. She'd show that lot.

She was just about to hop out of the car when the radio burst back to life.

'Ah, DS Freeman?' It was Wilson again.

She rolled her eyes. 'Yes, what is it? I haven't got all day.'

Wilson cleared his throat. 'That bus was found and returned to its owners three days ago.'

'What? How?' She could feel her face going red.

'Downsfordvale Station has been understaffed and so they sent some paperwork over for Barker and me and I just saw it on top of the pile,' Wilson admitted.

'And you haven't done it? What on God's earth have you been doing for the past three days? It's not as if we've been overrun. Now I have to go and tell them it was all just a stupid mistake – and thanks to you, I'll be doing it in front of a bus load of kids on their way to camp. I won't half be a laughing stock!' Fenella exploded.

It was just as well she couldn't see Wilson. Back in the station, he mimicked her perfectly, throwing his hands around and stomping his feet.

'Don't forget my coffee,' he said cheerily. Then again, he thought, judging by how cross Freeman sounded, she'd probably put poison in it.

Fenella slammed the car door. She took a deep breath, smoothed the front of her trousers and pushed back a rogue strand of hair.

'Well, what's going on?' Miss Reedy demanded as the officer strode towards them.

Fenella drew her shoulders back. 'It seems there has been a mix-up.'

'I knew it,' Miss Reedy said as Mr Plumpton sighed, his shoulders slumping as if he'd just been pricked by a pin. 'Mr Plumpton is not a criminal. He's a fine upstanding citizen.' She gave him a knowing smile, then reached out and grabbed his arm.

'How did it happen?' Mr Lipp asked, scowling.

'Someone forgot to remove the vehicle from the police database. Rest assured they will be disciplined for their appalling oversight.'

Harry Lipp eyeballed her. 'An apology would be nice.'

Fenella Freeman stared at his outfit. She wondered if he realised he was on school camp in Dunleavy, not on safari in Africa. He could shoot an elephant before she'd apologise. None of this was her fault.

'What's she saying?' Rufus asked as the students strained to hear what was going on.

'I think it's all been a mix-up,' Alice-Miranda called.

Half of the occupants of the bus sighed with relief while the other half groaned with disappointment.

'That's boring,' said one of the boys, curling his lip.

'Can I have a ride in the police car?' Figgy asked DS Freeman.

Miss Reedy shot the boy a frosty stare, bettered only by the terrifying look on the detective's face.

'You'd better get the children off to wherever it is that you're going. Enjoy your afternoon.' Fenella didn't look back as she stalked to the police car and hopped in. She revved the engine and spun the car around at speed, then roared out of the driveway.

'She didn't look very happy,' Alice-Miranda said to Millie as the teachers and Figgy hopped back on the bus.

'I'd say someone's going to *cop it* when she gets back to the station,' Sep said, a smile creeping across his face.

'Oh, that's lame.' Sloane shook her head.

Mr Plumpton turned the key in the ignition and the bus sputtered back to life.

'Well, I'm glad that ridiculous little fiasco is over,' Mr Lipp tutted.

'Yes, and I'll be happy not to meet another police officer for a very long time,' Mr Plumpton agreed.

Chapter 12

Mr Plumpton manoeuvred the minibus around the circular driveway just as the coaches were pulling out to leave. The children unpacked their belongings and carried them to a large quadrangle behind the manor. Miss Wall was barking orders into a loud-hailer, and for the moment Miss Reedy was more than happy to let her. According to the schedule, the children needed to be put into their groups, deposit their belongings in their dormitories and complete their first activities before dinner was served at 6 pm.

'I can't wait to find out what we're doing first,' Alice-Miranda said to Millie as they left their bags and ran to join the rest of the students.

Benitha Wall wasn't at all shy about using her loudhailer. 'Good afternoon, everyone. *So* glad that you could make it, Mr Plumpton,' Benitha Wall said into the loudhailer. She'd seen the minibus pulling into the driveway some time ago and wondered what was keeping them, until she spied the police car. 'Hope there wasn't any trouble getting here.' She couldn't wait to hear that story in the teachers' lounge after the children went to bed.

Josiah Plumpton's nose glowed and he took a sudden interest in his shoes.

Livinia Reedy walked to the front of the group to join Miss Wall. She whispered something to the PE teacher, who handed her the loudhailer.

'Good afternoon, everyone.' Miss Reedy spoke into the mouthpiece, which squawked loudly. She recoiled and Miss Wall indicated for her not to hold it so close.

'Goo-ood af-ter-noo-oon, Miss Ree-eedy,' the children chorused.

'As you are aware, we are on this camp because Queen Georgiana is introducing a new award for children your age. In order to achieve the first level of the award, you will need to complete a number of tasks, which will show your resilience, cooperation, ability to learn, friendship, application, courage, creativity and resourcefulness. Each time you complete a task to the standard required, the teacher in charge of your group will make a note that you have passed. Only those students who have passed a sufficient number of tasks will receive the Queen's Blue award. But as far as Miss Grimm and Professor Winterbottom are concerned, you must *all* earn your Blue. On top of that, we teachers will also be noting your attitude, ability and cooperative skills and nominating *one* Queen's Blue winner to receive a special medal from Queen Georgiana herself,' Miss Reedy explained.

Millie glanced over at Caprice, who had a very superior look on her face. Millie nudged Alice-Miranda and motioned towards Caprice. 'Three guesses who thinks she's going to win the medal.'

Alice-Miranda kept her eyes forward. 'It could be anyone,' she said emphatically. 'It could be you.'

Miss Reedy shuffled the papers in front of her. 'There will be a team competition too. Your rewards will be far less exciting but I imagine they will go down well all the same.' She pulled a packet of chocolate frogs from her bag.

A loud cheer went up around the quadrangle and Miss Reedy smiled. She motioned for Miss Wall to take the loudhailer back again.

'Would you read the camp groups please, Benitha? I think I'm required over there for a moment.' Miss Reedy nodded towards a huddle of uniformed camp instructors, where a young woman was waving.

'Okay, everyone.' Miss Wall scanned the list on the clipboard. 'I've got your camp groups and your sleeping groups. Generally they will be the same, except of course that the boys will have their own accommodation.'

The girls began to speculate about which group they would be in, grabbing the arms of friends as if that could magically change the list Miss Wall had in front of her.

'Settle down. There will be a camp instructor for each group and a teacher assigned to you as well. You need to make sure that you listen to the adults and do all that they ask of you. It's critical that you're in the right place at the right time doing the right thing. A camp timetable is posted in each dormitory and you'll all be given a smaller version to keep in your day pack,' Miss Wall explained. 'So without further delay, these are your camp groups.'

The children listened carefully. The groups were all named after birds. The new year three students, collectively called the Robins, were staying together to do a modified program, as they had only just come out of infants school and started at Winchesterfield-Downsfordvale. The older students, including the boys, were in mixed-age groups.

Alice-Miranda's name was the first to be read out for the Barn Owls. She squeezed Millie's hand nervously. Millie's was the next name called. Then came Sloane and Jacinta, Susannah, Lucas, Sep, Figgy and Rufus. Millie clenched her fist and hissed 'yesss' when she realised Caprice wasn't in their group. Their camp leader was a smiling, sandy-haired young woman called Beth, and their teacher was Mr Plumpton.

Miss Wall finished the announcements and a hand went up in the crowd. 'Yes?'

'I don't have a group, miss,' Caprice said sadly.

'Oh dear me, I am sorry about that,' the teacher apologised. 'What's your name?'

'Caprice Radford.'

'Oh, that's right. Your mother's Venetia Baldini. *Sweet Things* is one of my favourite shows,' Miss Wall babbled.

'Yes, yes, let's not make a fuss.' Miss Reedy hurried back over and scanned the lists. 'I was thinking about where to put her,' she whispered to Miss Wall. 'Sorry I hadn't written it down. She's a Barn Owl.'

Miss Wall nodded and turned back to the students. 'Here you are, Caprice. You're a Barn Owl.'

Millie's stomach flipped. She turned around and stared at Caprice, whose perfect face was now sporting the most perfect sneer.

The children began to fidget and chatter.

'Settle down, everyone. Before you go anywhere I need to tell you where you'll be sleeping. The girls' rooms are on the first and second floors of Bagley Hall and all of the boys are up in the attic. Gather up your belongings and head upstairs. And don't leave anything behind. You need to be back here in ten minutes with a water bottle and a jacket, ready for your first activities.'

Millie and Alice-Miranda turned around to get their things. Caprice had already disappeared.

'Hey, where's my sleeping bag?' Millie asked with a frown. She looked up and down.

'Perhaps someone picked it up by accident,' Alice-Miranda said. 'Don't worry, I'm sure we'll find it.'

Millie knew she'd left it right on top of her backpack. She and Alice-Miranda darted between the other students, searching, but had no luck.

'Come on, Millie, we'd better get upstairs.' Alice-Miranda grabbed her backpack and Millie followed. By the time they got to the second floor and found the barn owl on the door, the other girls were already there and had claimed their beds. The room had three sets of bunk beds and Sloane, Caprice and Jacinta were all sitting on top of them. Susannah was sitting on the bed under Caprice's.

'Hey, not fair,' Millie said. 'We should have flipped a coin for the top bunks.'

'You snooze, you lose,' said Caprice. 'I'm going to the toilet.' She grabbed her water bottle and jacket and leapt down from the top bunk.

The enormous room was sparsely furnished with three chests of drawers, three sets of bunks and a small lounge setting. And while the furniture was as plain as an arrowroot biscuit, the building itself was beautiful, with high ceilings, patterned cornices and rich, honey-coloured timber floors.

'Did anyone see my sleeping bag? It was on my backpack one minute and the next it was gone,' Millie explained.

The other girls shook their heads. A loud thump on the doorframe made them jump. Miss Wall stuck her head in and boomed, 'Downstairs in two minutes.'

The girls grabbed their water bottles and jackets from their bags and joined the throng of students rushing back to the quadrangle.

The groups lined up in front of their leaders, ready to hear the next set of instructions.

Miss Reedy walked to the podium and picked up the loudhailer.

'Goodness me, I am disappointed already,' she said, shaking her head. 'What did Miss Wall tell you about taking everything with you? When I came back outside, what did I find right there in the middle of the quadrangle, as plain as the nose on my face?'

Millie's chest felt tight.

Miss Reedy picked up the offending item and held it aloft for all to see.

'Millicent, come and get this, please. And if I find any more of your things lying about, you'll be on camp clean-up for the rest of the week,' the woman growled.

Millie's freckles were on fire as she skulked to the front and took the sleeping bag from Miss Reedy's hand.

'Sorry, Miss Reedy,' she said quietly.

'Just don't let it happen again,' the teacher said.

As Millie turned to walk back to the group she caught sight of Caprice smiling.

'She took it,' Millie whispered to Alice-Miranda.

Alice-Miranda turned around to look at Caprice, who was now giving Miss Reedy her full attention.

'You don't know that,' Alice-Miranda said.

'You didn't see the way she was smiling when I got into trouble,' said Millie.

Benitha Wall handed the groups over to their leaders, who were going to explain their first activity.

'Hello everyone, I'm Beth and I'm going to be with you for the next week. You all know Mr Plumpton, I'm sure,' she said, smiling at the teacher beside her.

'Go, Mr P,' Figgy called. 'You're a legend, sir, best bus driver ever.' He winked at Mr Plumpton, who blushed.

'Figworth, be quiet or we'll never get started,' the Science teacher said with a scowl.

Beth stepped in. 'I hope you all like finding treasure, because that's your first activity. I want you to work in pairs. You will each receive the first clue and a map of the grounds – don't stray outside of the boundaries. You'll be looking for numbered treasure tokens. When you find them, make sure you take the token showing the lowest number, as the pair with the least points at the end will be the winners. Once you have your token, look around for a box. It will contain the next clue. You've got forty-five minutes to find the five items and bring your tokens back to me. Choose your fellow hunter and let's see how good you are at figuring things out,' Beth explained. She walked around handing out the maps and the first clue.

'Is everyone doing the treasure hunt?' Figgy asked.

'No, just our group. The others are out riding bikes or playing games in the indoor sports hall. There are two groups doing archery and I think some of the others are going for a long walk.'

'Is there a prize?' Figgy asked.

'I have some camp currency you might enjoy,' Beth replied.

'What's that?' Figgy had no idea.

'I think she means sweets,' Alice-Miranda said.

Beth smiled at her and nodded.

Alice-Miranda paired up with Millie and Jacinta chose Sloane. Sep and Lucas formed another pair, leaving Susannah, Caprice, Rufus and Figgy still sorting things out.

'Do you want to be my partner?' Figgy grinned at Caprice and wiggled his eyebrows.

'I'd rather eat camp food,' the girl retorted.

Figgy looked crestfallen. 'You don't have to be mean about it.'

Caprice stood beside Susannah. 'I suppose it's you and me then.'

'Don't sound so excited,' Susannah said with a frown.

'I didn't mean it like that,' Caprice replied sweetly. 'I'm glad you're my partner.'

Beth pulled a stopwatch out of her pocket. 'Okay, I'm putting you on the clock. On your marks, get set, go!' she called, and the children scattered in all directions.

Chapter 13

Fenella Freeman drummed her fingers on the steering wheel. Her foot was planted firmly on the accelerator as she zoomed towards town. As the car entered the roundabout just before the village shops, she changed her mind, steered a full circle and drove back along the same road. If Wilson thought she was still bringing his coffee, he was even thicker than she'd first thought. She needed to talk to someone. And while she didn't always see eye to eye with her father, he was a pretty good listener.

Fenella turned left into Pelham Park's long driveway. Her father had spent much of his childhood in a cottage on the estate, as his own father had once been the butler. It sounded like an idyllic life, with lots of children to play with and grounds to roam about. Fenella's father learned how to fish and hunt and she'd heard stories of his great adventures.

But when her father was fifteen years old, her grandfather's employment was terminated. Her father had never told her why. All she knew was that her grandfather, her grandmother and their four children – the eldest of whom was Fenella's father – were booted from the estate, at a time when jobs were scarce and life was tough. It was the undoing of her grandfather, who never recovered from the setback. He died in his early forties. Her grandmother struggled on, but it never got any easier and she too died at a young age. Losing their livelihood and home had been a tremendous blow.

Despite his early difficulties, Fenella's father earned a law degree and became a doting husband and father. He developed a passion for art and shared this love with his children, often taking Fenella and her brother, Niall, to galleries to see his favourite paintings. When Fenella's mother became ill, her father stopped working and cared for her until she passed away.

Seven years ago, when Pelham Park was transformed into an aged-care home, Fenella was stunned that her father decided to purchase one of the self-contained apartments. He could have lived anywhere, but he insisted that he was tired of living alone and wanted to be among people his own age. Fenella had wondered if it was her father's perverse way of getting his own back. His family had been kicked off the estate but now he was going to buy part of the mansion and no one would be able to tell him to leave. After what the Kennington-Joneses had done to her grandfather, she really couldn't understand it at all.

She pulled into a vacant parking spot at the side of the building and hopped out of the car. Pelham Park was a beautiful building, with double-storey bay windows and a rooftop colonnade. The honey-coloured stone was pretty but there was something overbearing about the place that Fenella couldn't quite put her finger on.

She buzzed herself through the front doors and into the majestic timber-panelled entrance hall.

'Good afternoon, DS Freeman,' a sunshiny voice called from afar.

Fenella plastered a smile on her face. 'Good afternoon, matron,' she replied.

'Come to see your father?' The woman almost trilled, such was the sing-song nature of her voice.

Fenella wanted to tell her that she'd come to investigate a murder, just to shake the old bird up a bit. Matron Bright asked the same question every time she saw her and every time the answer was the same. What did the woman think she was there for?

Fenella resisted the temptation to embellish the reason for her visit. 'Yes, how is he?'

'You know your father. He's a happy chap,' the woman said and bounced away.

Matron Marigold Bright was one of those people Fenella found unreasonably irritating. She'd never slighted Fenella and was inordinately kind to her father, yet Fenella could barely stand to be in the same room as the woman. Unkind thoughts sprang immediately to mind. And not just about her. The whole staff seemed to be made of up of strange people who spent their entire lives smiling, as if looking after a house full of geriatrics and a nursing home wing where most of the residents had forgotten their own names, was something to look forward to each day.

Her own career may have hit a rough spot, but Fenella would prefer to chase criminals any day of the week, even on wild goose chases like the one she'd just had.

The afternoon sun streamed through the stained-glass windows on the stairwell, lending more colour to the brightly patterned runner. Fenella walked up to the first floor. She wondered how on earth just one family ever lived in such a ludicrously large house. Nowadays there were thirty good-sized apartments on the first floor alone, each with a bedroom, sitting room, kitchen and bathroom. Her father resided halfway along one of the hallways in the left wing. She rang the buzzer and waited for him to answer.

The old man opened the door. 'Hello Fen, you home from school already?' he said as she walked through.

Fenella clenched her jaw. 'Dad, I'm not at school any more. Remember?'

Donald looked at his daughter. He paused for a few moments. 'Oh, of course, I was just kidding, you know.'

But Fenella wasn't so sure. There had been several occasions recently when he'd asked her about school or if her mum would be home from the shops soon. She was starting to worry about him.

'I was close by and thought I'd pop in for a cuppa. Not busy, are you?'

'No, not at all, love. Matron Bright brought me up a slice of cake. I can share it with you,' he offered.

'Of course she did,' Fenella muttered as she followed her father into the sitting room.

Donald continued into the kitchen but something on the dining room table caught his daughter's eye. A stunning oil painting, as yet unframed. She walked over to inspect it more closely and marvelled at the movement of the horses as they thundered down the track. She glanced at the signature in the bottom right-hand corner and sighed.

'I was going to give you a ring. My radio's on the blink and I wondered if you could get me a new one next time you're at the shops,' Donald called.

'Yeah, sure,' Fenella replied. Then she thought for a moment. 'Actually, I think I might have a spare one at home.'

'That'd be perfect, love,' Donald replied.

He filled the kettle, located two mugs and scooped three heaped spoons of tea into a battered silver pot.

'Your brother telephoned this morning,' he said. 'His new exhibition is doing wonderfully well. He and Sophie and the children send their love.'

'That's nice,' Fenella mumbled. As children Fenella and Niall had been close, but when her brother won a competition that propelled his career into the stratosphere, their relationship changed. Niall moved to France, met Sophie and was busy being one of the world's most sought-after artists.

Her father reappeared and set a tea tray on the table. He quickly rolled up the painting and placed it to the side.

'Did you look at it?' he said, nodding towards the art.

'Mmm. Perfect as always.' There was a tinge of resentment in her voice.

'Are you all right, Fen?' Donald asked as he began to pour the tea.

'No, not really.' Fenella added some milk.

'It can't be as bad as all that, can it?'

'I need a case, Dad. A proper case. If I'm ever going to get out of here and work my way up the ladder I can't be investigating stolen vehicles that have already been returned to their owners. That pair of imbeciles I work with have no idea,' Fenella blathered.

Her father offered her a slice of cake. 'Why don't you quit the Force and do something else, while you're still young.'

'Really? Like what?' Fenella snapped.

'Like that.' The old man pointed at the rolled-up painting. 'You've got more talent in your little finger than your brother and look at how well he's doing.'

'Stop it, Dad. You know why I joined the police – because I failed at that thing I was supposed to be so good at.'

'You didn't fail, Fen. A couple of bad reviews and you threw it all away.' Donald Freeman stared at his daughter.

'I don't want to talk about it. I'm a detective. A really good one, but I can't spend the rest of my days chasing crimes that don't exist,' Fenella snapped.

'Well, you know how I feel about it,' her father said.

'Yes, and it's a bit rich coming from you. How many years did you spend as a criminal lawyer?'

'But I never represented anyone I didn't think deserved my help,' the old man insisted.

It was true that Donald Freeman had never taken on the worst of the worst. There were no murderers or violent criminals on his books. But there was a long line of thieves – so many so, that his nickname around the traps had been 'Fagin'. It was a constant source of tension between him and Fenella. Even now in his retirement he'd frequently take up the cause of the criminals. His argument was that people weren't necessarily born bad, but that often circumstances meant that they had to do some bad things to survive.

Fenella didn't agree and lived by the motto 'Commit the crime, do the time.'

'Well, I'm sure something will come up soon.' Donald nodded thoughtfully and took a sip of his tea.

Fenella picked up her mug. 'I hope you're right, Dad. I hope you're right.'

Chapter 14

Alice-Miranda studied the first clue.

'"Tie a yellow ribbon round the *blank blank blank*." Three words.'

'Huh?' Millie frowned. 'What's that supposed to mean? Have you seen any yellow ribbons anywhere? What are we supposed to tie it around?'

'It's a song,' Alice-Miranda replied. '"Tie a Yellow Ribbon Round the Old Oak Tree".'

'How would you know that?' Millie asked. 'Seriously, Alice-Miranda, sometimes I think there must be a fifty-year-old woman trapped in that eight-year-old body of yours.'

'I've heard it on the radio. Mrs Oliver listens to an old-fashioned station. Some of the songs are terrible but some are pretty catchy. Now we've just got to find an oak tree.'

The girls spun around, scanning the garden and the fields.

'What about them?' Millie pointed at the driveway, which was lined by large trees.

Alice-Miranda shook her head. 'Plane trees.'

'Oh, I thought they were sort of pretty,' Millie said.

Alice-Miranda giggled. 'I don't mean *plain* as in *dull*. They're called plane trees, the same spelling as aeroplane. It's just their name.'

Millie grinned. 'I think I need some gardening lessons from Charlie. What about around the back?'

The two girls scooted off to see what they could find.

Caprice had also figured out the answer, but she and Susannah had gone in the opposite direction and found themselves near the gymnasium. They were heading back to the front of the house when Susannah spotted Alice-Miranda and Millie.

'We should follow them,' Susannah suggested. 'Alice-Miranda is the smartest person I've ever met.'

'Until now, maybe,' Caprice retorted, then raced in the girls' direction.

'There!' Alice-Miranda pointed. A lush canopy of leaves rose above a high wall. 'On the other side.'

She and Millie ran towards the rear garden, past a volleyball court and some sheds, with Caprice and Susannah hot on their heels.

They rounded the garden wall and found a climbing course. Right in the middle with a rope bridge attached was a giant oak tree.

'There it is,' Caprice shouted and sprinted towards the tree. The girls had to find a token and they wanted the one labelled '1', to show they were the first to solve the puzzle.

Millie chased after her as fast as she could. 'Number one is ours!' she shouted.

Caprice reached the tree, puffing and blowing. Her eyes searched for the tokens. But Millie spotted them first and snatched the small circular disc bearing a '1'.

'What?' Give me that!' Caprice demanded.

Millie shook her head. 'No. I saw it first.'

Susannah and Alice-Miranda reached the tree.

'I'll get the next clue,' said Alice-Miranda. She ran to look for the box that Beth had explained would contain the next clue. Susannah spotted it sitting on top of a post that formed the start of the low ropes course. She bolted towards it and opened the lid, handing Alice-Miranda an envelope before taking another for herself.

'Why are you helping her?' Caprice bellowed.

Susannah looked sheepish. 'Sorry,' she mumbled. 'But we're friends and friends help each other.'

'Not when it's a competition, they don't.' Caprice snatched the clue from Susannah's hand and charged around the corner of the wall. 'Are you coming or not?' she screeched.

'Sorry, Alice-Miranda,' said Susannah. 'I hadn't realised it was that big a deal.'

'It's not,' Millie said. 'Except to *her*.'

Alice-Miranda opened the envelope and read the clue aloud. '"I am frozen to the spot to view my domain."'

'What's that supposed to mean?' Millie asked.

'Think about it. What can be frozen?' Alice-Miranda asked.

'Um, an ice block,' Millie replied.

'Yes, but I don't think the cook will want us raiding the freezer,' Alice-Miranda said as she studied the map of the grounds.

'What about a statue?' Millie asked.

'Of course!' Alice-Miranda's eyes widened. 'But where? Did you see anything out the front?'

Millie shook her head.

Alice-Miranda tucked the map into her pocket and grabbed Millie's hand. The girls took off running towards the quadrangle.

'Didn't it say something about "surveying my domain"?' Alice-Miranda asked as the girls reached the little raised platform where the teachers gave their announcements.

'So we're looking for somewhere high. The statue must overlook something,' Millie agreed.

The group's camp leader, Beth, was walking towards the girls.

'Hi there,' she called. 'Have you had any luck?'

'Yes, we found the oak tree but now we think we're looking for a statue,' Millie said. 'Is that right?'

Beth winked. 'I can't tell you that. It wouldn't be fair.'

Figgy and Rufus rounded the corner. 'Have you found anything yet?' Figgy called.

Millie nodded. 'Sure have. We're looking for the second clue.'

Rufus looked crestfallen. 'We haven't even worked out the first one yet. Can we phone a friend?'

Beth walked over to the boys. 'Come on, tell me what you're thinking and I'll see if you're on the right track.'

'Over there!' Alice-Miranda shouted and pointed to the other side of the quadrangle.

'What are you looking at?' Millie couldn't see any statues.

'In the garden.' Alice-Miranda hotfooted it across the pavement.

Millie ran after her but still couldn't understand what she was looking at. A statue should have been obvious, like the enormous ones in the gardens at Alice-Miranda's house.

Down among the shrubs was a gnome. Taped to his little hat were five tokens.

'That's not what I was looking for,' Millie said with a grin. 'He looks like Mrs Parker's gnome, Newton. He probably stowed away on the bus with us, just to get away from her. You know he likes to travel.'

'Poor Newton. I don't think Mrs Parker lets him outside at all these days,' Alice-Miranda said with a giggle.

She reached in and picked off the token marked '1' while Millie searched for the box containing the next clue.

She located it at the back of the garden and pulled out an envelope just as Jacinta and Sloane arrived to take the second token.

'Have you seen Caprice and Susannah?' Millie asked.

'They were down the back near the tennis courts,' Sloane gasped. 'We thought we'd be last to get here. We were number four at the tree.'

'I'm glad you beat Caprice,' Millie said. 'She tried to snatch our number last time. She's going to be really mad when she realises she's at least third to get here.'

Millie opened their envelope and she and Alice-Miranda sped away to read the clue: 'Peter Rabbit's favourite food.'

'This one's easy,' Millie said. She was starting to get the hang of the clues and remembered straight away that she'd seen a vegetable patch marked next to the tennis courts on the map. Somewhere among the carrots they would find the next clue.

The girls sprinted towards the tennis courts, passing Caprice and Susannah on the way.

'Have you found the second clue?' Susannah asked.

Millie nodded.

Caprice's eyes were wild. 'Stop talking to them!' She grabbed Susannah's hand and dragged her around the corner. 'You go and get the next clue. I've got a stone in my shoe,' she whined.

Susannah did what she was told. Sep and Lucas had just pulled the third token from the gnome, leaving Susannah to collect the fourth.

Susannah came back with the next clue.

'What number did you get?' Caprice demanded.

Susannah reluctantly held up four fingers.

'Argh!' Caprice clenched her fist and shuddered. 'They can't win. I won't let them!' She snatched the clue from Susannah and tore it open.

'Easy!' she blurted. She started for the vegetable patch, where she'd seen Millie and Alice-Miranda heading. There'd been no stone in her shoe at all. She'd just wanted to see which direction the girls went.

Millie and Alice-Miranda had found the patch easily enough but the treasure was proving more difficult.

Susannah followed Caprice as she ran through the tomatoes and sunflowers.

'There!' Caprice pointed at a basket of carrots covered in numbers.

Millie was watching from a few beds away. She grabbed Alice-Miranda's hand and the girls raced towards Susannah and Caprice, but Caprice had already taken the first token and found the next clue.

'So, still think you're the smartest girls in the school?' Caprice taunted.

Millie pulled a face. 'You haven't won yet.'

'Oh, but I will,' Caprice promised and darted off to open the clue.

'How much time do we have left?' Millie asked.

Alice-Miranda glanced at her watch. 'About twelve minutes to solve the last two clues.'

The fourth clue proved trickier than all the others and turned out to be the shed where the canoes and kayaks were stored. Somehow Lucas and Sep managed to get there first, leaving Caprice and Susannah with the second token and Alice-Miranda and Millie in third place.

The race to the finish was neck and neck.

'Quick, what's the clue?' Millie's heart hammered inside her chest. She wanted to beat Caprice more than she'd wanted anything for a very long time.

'"The spring is in the water",' Alice-Miranda read. 'I've got it!' She grabbed Millie's hand and charged off.

'Where are we going?' Millie shouted.

'The indoor pool,' Alice-Miranda puffed. 'If there's a diving board I think that's what we're looking for.'

'We could lock the others out,' Millie said.

'But that would be cheating.' Alice-Miranda gave her friend a playful shove as they ran along the path they thought would take them to the pool.

Caprice had figured out the clue too and was bolting after them. As Alice-Miranda and Millie neared the building, they looked for the entrance. There was a lot of glass and the location of the doors wasn't clear.

'I'll go the other way,' Millie panted. She took the path that led right while Alice-Miranda went left.

'Go left!' Caprice barked at Susannah.

The poor girl wasn't keen to be on the sharp end of Caprice's tongue again and did exactly as she was told. Caprice raced after Millie just as the red-haired girl found the door and pushed it open.

'No!' Caprice screeched and followed Millie inside. Caprice spun around and looked at the door, then reached out and turned the latch.

Millie scanned the pool deck. Sure enough, a diving board jutted out across the water. She ran for it. There were five tokens on the ladder. Millie reached out to take the first one.

'No!' Caprice shouted. She was right behind her. 'No, no, no! That's mine.' She stamped her foot like a two-year-old.

'Caprice, it's a game,' Millie snapped.

'But I don't lose anything!' Caprice snarled, poking Millie sharply in the chest.

'Too bad, you just did.'

Outside, Alice-Miranda and Susannah finally located the door only to find it locked. Alice-Miranda wondered how that had happened and pushed the thought of Millie's earlier comment about the pool out of her head. Why would she lock the door with Caprice already inside? The girls ran to find Mr Plumpton or Beth.

Inside, Caprice and Millie were still arguing. 'Give me that token,' Caprice demanded.

Millie shook her head.

Caprice's eyes narrowed. 'Give it to me. Or else.'

'Or else what? You'll push me in the pool?' Millie laughed at her. 'Seriously, it's just a game. As long as you complete the task, you'll pass.'

'But I don't want to pass. I want to be first. Besides, how could I push you in the pool when I'm the one with my back to it?'

Millie had begun to wonder if there was something seriously wrong with Caprice. Competitive wasn't the half of it.

Caprice was watching over Millie's shoulder. She waited until she could see Alice-Miranda and the teachers come into view near the doors.

'Stop it, Millie, stop pushing me,' she yelled as loudly as she could.

Millie looked at the girl, bewildered.

Caprice stepped backwards, edging closer and closer to the water.

'What are you doing?' Millie demanded.

'You'll see,' Caprice snapped. She could see Beth and Mr Plumpton through the glass.

Beth was fumbling with the key on the lanyard around her neck.

'Stop it! Don't touch me!' Caprice screeched at the top of her voice.

'I'm not touching you,' Millie said. 'Are you hallucinating?'

'No, of course not,' Caprice hissed. 'You know, I don't think you deserve to pass this test, after what you did to me.'

'What did I do to you?' Millie said. 'Come away from the edge.'

'Why? Are you worried I might fall in?' Caprice pouted.

'Oh, for goodness sake.' Millie lunged at the girl and grabbed for her arm. Just as she did, there was a loud splash as Caprice toppled backwards into the water.

Outside, Beth finally managed to unlock the door. Mr Plumpton ran towards the pool while Beth raced to fetch a lifebuoy.

'Oh heavens, Caprice, I'm coming!' Mr Plumpton kicked off his shoes and leapt into the water, clothes and all. He sank like a stone, before pushing off the bottom of the pool and snatching the child under one arm. The pair burst to the surface, coughing and spluttering.

Caprice seemed to be fighting Mr Plumpton all the way and the poor man struggled to keep his head above the water.

'Here, grab this.' Beth threw the lifebuoy, which the teacher caught.

The young woman hauled and heaved the sodden pair to the ladder, before grabbing Caprice and pulling her out of the water.

'Are you all right, Mr Plumpton?' asked Alice-Miranda. She handed the teacher a stripy beach towel that she'd found close by. His clothes were stuck to his body like soggy cling wrap.

Jacinta and Sloane arrived just as the boys all got there too.

'What happened?' Rufus asked. 'Did you forget your togs, sir?'

'Does it look like I meant to go swimming, Pemberley?' the man snapped as he peeled off his jacket.

Caprice was snivelling and shivering. 'She . . . she pushed me.' She pointed at Millie.

'I did not!' Millie felt her temperature rising.

'You saw it, didn't you, Mr Plumpton?' Caprice sobbed. 'You all saw it. I was just trying to get away and she pushed me in.'

'Well, it did look like that.' Mr Plumpton nodded slowly.

Millie's face was incredulous.

'She locked the door too,' Caprice wailed.

'That's a lie!' Millie scoffed. 'She's lying!'

'Millie, settle down. The last thing we need is for you to lose your temper. I think we'll have to discuss with Miss Reedy whether you'll pass this activity. We can't have dangerous behaviour – Caprice might have drowned,' said Mr Plumpton, shaking his head – although the children couldn't tell if it was because he was upset with Millie or he was trying to get the water out of his ears.

'She wouldn't have drowned. I'm sure she can swim perfectly well.' Millie's lip trembled but she was determined not to cry.

'My clothes were so heavy,' Caprice said with a sniffle. 'I thought I was going to die.'

'Oh, give it a rest, Caprice. You're disgusting!' Millie stomped off. 'I don't care about the stupid treasure hunt.'

'Millie!' said Alice-Miranda, and went after her friend.

Beth looked at the rest of the children. 'Come on, we'll go back to the quadrangle and get your tokens sorted out.' But the shine had gone off the treasure.

'Caprice, you can go back to the house and get changed. Susannah, would you go with her please?' Mr Plumpton instructed.

Susannah nodded. She didn't want to believe that Millie pushed Caprice. But from where she stood, it certainly looked that way.

Chapter 15

'It's not fair,' Millie grouched as she scraped left-overs into the bin. 'Why do I have to do extra kitchen duty when Caprice planned to fall in the pool all along? She's evil.'

Alice-Miranda stood on a little rubber-topped stool and pulled the trigger on the giant snake-like tap. She rinsed the smeared plates before stacking them in the oversized dishwasher tray beside her.

'Don't worry about Caprice,' Alice-Miranda said. She wondered why the girl had it in for Millie.

Alice-Miranda believed what Millie told her about the pool incident. It was a pity that Mr Plumpton and Miss Reedy didn't. 'Caprice is probably lonely. Maybe she just wants some friends.'

'I know you're right about a lot of things, Alice-Miranda, but this time you're wrong,' Millie said. 'I don't think she knows the first thing about being a friend. She just wants to win everything.'

Livinia Reedy poked her head into the kitchen to see how the girls were getting on. She'd been very surprised to hear about what happened at the pool, but Beth and Mr Plumpton had both seen it and, despite Millie's protests, it seemed that the girl had lost her temper and deliberately pushed Caprice in. Livinia wondered if Millie was jealous. Caprice was terribly clever and talented, not to mention stunning. She was one of those rare souls who seemed to have it all. It was only natural that she'd gravitate towards Alice-Miranda, who was probably the closest to her intellectual equal in the school.

'Are you managing with all that?' Miss Reedy asked.

'Oh, hello Miss Reedy.' Alice-Miranda smiled at the woman. 'Yes, we're almost done.'

Millie looked into the bin and had to stop herself from gagging. Gelatinous lumps of gravy were mixed in with soggy peas, grey mashed potato and the odd fleck of orange carrot as well as chunks of jelly and sticky white liquid that had once been ice-cream.

'After dinner, Millie, you can go straight up to your room,' Miss Reedy said.

'But that's not fair. I've already done extra duties and I didn't push Caprice in the pool in the first place,' Millie protested.

'We'll talk about it later when you're upstairs,' said Miss Reedy.

'But Miss Reedy,' Millie complained.

'Millie, I want to believe you. I really do. But some of the things I've seen and heard from you since Caprice arrived have given me cause for concern.'

'Can't you see? She's setting me up,' Millie fumed.

'Really? You have been known to lose your temper,' the teacher reminded her.

'When?' Millie demanded.

'I remember a rather unpleasant incident with a bowl of dessert on Sloane's head.'

'Oh, that.' Millie picked up the last plate and gave it her full attention.

Miss Reedy nodded. 'Yes, *that*. I'll come up and see you before the other girls go to bed.'

'May I stay with Millie?' Alice-Miranda asked.

'No, you have choir practice,' Miss Reedy said. 'Mr Lipp needs you there.'

'I'm in the choir too,' Millie reminded the woman.

'Yes, and you're sitting this one out to reflect on how you're going to make things work with Caprice.' Miss Reedy stared at Millie pointedly and then walked out of the kitchen.

Millie shrugged. 'I don't know what she wants me to reflect on. Caprice hates me.'

'I'm sure she doesn't hate you,' Alice-Miranda said. 'Maybe you should ask her if you can have a chat and sort things out. I'll talk to her too.'

'But I didn't do anything wrong,' Millie grumbled. 'It was her fault.'

Alice-Miranda rinsed the last plate. She pulled off the disposable rubber gloves and washed her hands for good measure, then walked over and gave Millie a hug.

'It's all right. Caprice is just finding her way. And you – you're Millie. You can do anything,' Alice-Miranda reassured her friend.

'Thanks.' Millie hugged Alice-Miranda back. 'I don't know what I'd ever do without you.'

☆

The next morning, Alice-Miranda placed the book she'd been reading into her backpack.

'What are you taking?' Millie asked.

'I'm hooked on *Black Beauty* at the moment. It's like reading the anti-Bonaparte story. I live in hope that one day my little monster will be as well behaved as Beauty,' she explained.

Millie grinned. 'Don't hold your breath.' She stuffed a dog-eared copy of *The Witches* into her pack and snatched her water bottle from the bed.

The previous evening Millie had spent an hour on her own before the other girls returned. As promised, Miss Reedy had come to talk to her. The teacher said that she understood that sometimes girls didn't get on, but asked her what she thought Alice-Miranda would do in the same situation.

That was easy. Alice-Miranda had been in Alethea Goldsworthy's sights from the minute she had arrived at Winchesterfield-Downsfordvale. And what did she do? She almost killed her with kindness and, even though Alethea had left the school, Alice-Miranda could hold her head high.

Miss Reedy asked Millie what sort of girl she'd rather be like – Alethea or Alice-Miranda. That was easy too. Heaven help anyone who actually wanted to be like Alethea. Millie decided she'd try to make peace with Caprice, even though she was one of those girls who always made sure that the teachers were out of earshot before she did anything mean. She could only try.

Miss Reedy said that, providing there were no more incidents, Millie would pass the activity. She was relieved to hear it.

When the girls arrived back at their dorm for the night, Millie told Caprice she was sorry about what happened. Truthfully she was, but she didn't add that she was sorry that Caprice had set her up and sorry that she had to miss choir and do extra kitchen duties. To everyone's surprise, Caprice accepted her apology.

Alice-Miranda had approached Caprice in the bathroom when they were brushing their teeth. Caprice had promised that there were no hard feelings and assured the younger girl that things were fine between her and Millie. Alice-Miranda hoped that was true.

So far that morning there hadn't been a cross word spoken and breakfast had been a cheery affair. Even the food seemed to taste better. There was cereal followed by pancakes with maple syrup and weak milky tea, just the way Millie liked it.

After breakfast, Beth and Mr Plumpton were waiting for the group out the front of Bagley Hall.

'When are we going rock climbing, sir?' Figgy asked as the boys arrived.

'If you look on your timetable, George, I'm sure you'll see that for yourself,' Mr Plumpton replied.

'Yeah, but you could just tell me,' Figgy said. 'Save me getting it out again.'

'Figworth, you do realise that this camp is about resourcefulness and independence?' Mr Plumpton reminded the lad.

Figgy nodded.

'And do you think asking me for the answers is displaying resourcefulness and independence?'

'Yeah, of course,' Figgy said. 'I'm resourceful because I ask someone who knows.'

The Science teacher shook his head and the children all giggled. 'I give up,' Mr Plumpton said.

'So how long do we have to go and visit the oldies for?' Sloane asked.

News that the children would be spending part of each day next door at the Pelham Park aged-care facility hadn't exactly sent shivers of excitement tingling through their veins. Except for Alice-Miranda. She couldn't wait to get over and see everyone.

'Sloane, I hope you will not be using that language in front of the residents,' Mr Plumpton admonished.

'What, "oldies"? Of course not.' The girl rolled her eyes. 'As if I'd be that rude.'

'We will be there for at least two hours each day, which will give you time to get to know people and read to them. The matron at Pelham Park has also suggested that some of you write down the stories the residents tell you, if they consent. Quite a few of them or their parents worked or lived on the estate, and the home is keen to record their memories for the anniversary fair. Other students will be assigned to help the matron with some preparations for the fair as well as some gardening duties. I expect all of you to be on your very best behaviour.'

At that moment there was a loud rumble followed by peals of laughter. A pall of pungent gas stung the children's eyes and the group wailed in disgust.

'You're rank, Figgy!' Rufus bellowed, holding his nose.

'What? Don't blame me. It was her.' The boy pointed at a cow grazing in the field. The old girl looked up and mooed.

Mr Plumpton shook his head. 'I'd advise you to cut back on the baked beans, Figworth. So much for best behaviour.'

The children giggled.

Chapter 16

Matron Bright had spent the morning rounding up a small group of the residents, who were now awaiting further instructions in the reading room.

'Good morning, everyone.' She bustled to the front, her voice trilling like a lark.

A chorus of good mornings echoed.

'What's all this about?' an elderly gentleman at the back called.

The matron beamed. 'You are quite the impatient

one this morning, Mr Mobbs. If you give me a minute I will explain.'

'I've got things to do, you know,' the man persisted.

'Yes, yes, but I was hoping you might like to help me this morning. The home shopping channel runs twenty-four hours a day and I doubt you or any of the other residents need another vacuum cleaner.'

'Oh, I do,' Mrs Von Thripp piped up.

Deep creases formed above Mr Mobbs's bushy eyebrows. Matron didn't know what she was talking about. He hadn't planned to buy any more vacuum cleaners. It was an ab cruncher he was after.

'Mrs Von Thripp, I don't think you've done any vacuuming since you moved into Pelham Park as a resident, have you, dear?' Matron Bright reminded the woman.

'I was vacuuming the master's bedroom just yesterday,' the grey-haired woman declared, nodding fiercely.

'I think that was a while ago. Mr Henry Kennington-Jones has been gone for a very long time now, but your apartment *does* occupy what was once his bedroom and dressing rooms, so I can see how you might get that confused,' the matron explained.

Mrs Von Thripp pursed her lips. And then, as if a light was suddenly switched on, she remembered. 'Oh, of course. I was Mr Kennington-Jones's maid, all those years ago when Hugh was just a little boy.'

The matron smiled at her. 'Good girl. Now, the reason you're all here this morning is that I have some lovely news. We are going to have some visitors over the next week.'

'I hate visitors,' a man with a curly moustache called out. 'They eat my cake.'

'No, no Mr Johnson, I can assure you that these visitors won't be eating your cake. They will be reading to you and writing down some of your stories, so that we can make a book of recollections of your lives here at Pelham Park.'

Most of the residents murmured their approval of this.

'Who are the visitors?' Mrs Von Thripp asked.

'They are students from the area's two finest schools. They are currently involved in a program that has been set out by none other than Her Majesty, Queen Georgiana,' Matron Bright explained.

Mr Mobbs nodded. 'Ooh, I like her. She's got class, that woman, and I've won a few bob on her horses over the years. But I don't like children. They smell.'

Marigold Bright suppressed the urge to laugh. It never ceased to amaze her that perfectly polite human beings frequently reached an age where they acquired what she had come to describe as the gift of natural rudeness. They didn't mean to be unkind, but they no longer cared what anyone really thought. It was as if they'd been injected with a truth serum of the brutally honest blend.

'What do you think, Mr Freeman?' she asked the man in the middle of the front row.

'It sounds all right to me,' Donald replied.

'Good. Well, the first group will be coming over in about twenty minutes. Some of the children will be chatting with you while others are going to the nursing home wing to do some reading. A few others will be helping me get things organised for the fair. I believe there's a group on gardening duty too.'

'What fair?' a voice called from the back of the room.

'The anniversary fair that we have on the weekend – the same one we have every year to celebrate Pelham Park's establishment, Mr Biggles,' Matron Bright said patiently. She never minded repeating herself and hoped that one day when she was old and a little bit forgetful someone would take the time to do the same for her.

☆

The Barn Owls set off down the driveway and along the road to the Pelham Park entrance.

The front of the estate was partially shielded by a high hedge, but once the children were inside the gates it was easy to see the full expanse of the main building.

Just as the group rounded the bend at the top of the driveway, a silver Range Rover pulled up in the car park.

Jacinta pointed and nudged Alice-Miranda. 'Isn't that your mother's car?'

Alice-Miranda looked at it. A huge smile spread across her face and she dashed towards the vehicle. 'Mummy! What are you doing here?'

Cecelia Highton-Smith hopped out of the passenger's seat and embraced her small daughter.

'Hello darling. I don't suppose you expected to see us.' She planted a kiss on Alice-Miranda's cheek.

The rear passenger door opened and Alice-Miranda almost jumped out of her skin. 'Uncle Ed!' She leapt into the man's arms. Ed Clifton scooped her up and Alice-Miranda kissed his soft cheek. She hugged him tightly.

'If I'd have known this was the way I'd be received I would have come months ago.' Ed smiled at Alice-Miranda and set her back down.

Hugh Kennington-Jones strode around the back of the vehicle and Alice-Miranda ran to hug him too.

'What are you all doing here?' she asked, her eyes sparkling with excitement.

'We'll tell you about it later, darling. I think you need to go.' Cecelia had noticed Mr Plumpton tapping his foot.

'We're starting our community service,' Alice-Miranda said. She glanced over at her group.

'Run along, sweetheart, and we'll catch up with you inside,' Cecelia instructed. 'You don't want to keep everyone waiting, do you?'

Alice-Miranda ran back to Millie. 'Isn't that a lovely surprise?'

Ed Clifton watched the children walk through the arched portico that framed the mansion's front door.

He stared up at the facade, remembering the last time he had seen it – the night he'd walked down the driveway to the waiting taxi at the gate. It had taken him to a new life, far from here.

Hugh watched his brother, wondering how he was going to cope with being back. 'Are you all right, Ed?'

'I'm fine. It's just strange. When I left I expected to come back some day – but I didn't realise it would take me almost forty years,' Ed said.

Cecelia linked arms with her brother-in-law. 'I telephoned Matron Bright this morning to let her know we were coming. She said that it was probably a good thing that the children would be keeping the residents busy this morning. Some of them may have known you as a boy and it might come as a shock,' she explained.

Ed nodded. 'My not being dead and all.'

'You'll love Marigold,' said Hugh. 'She's just what this place needed. I've never known anyone who actually beams like a ray of sunshine.'

'I don't know about that. Alice-Miranda would have to come close,' Ed said.

'We'll go around to the back door and avoid the crowd,' said Hugh.

'Lead the way, little brother,' Ed agreed. Cecelia looped her arm into Ed's and the pair followed.

'Welcome, everyone, come through,' Marigold Bright greeted the children as they walked into the Great Hall.

'Cool house,' Figgy said loudly.

'Thank you, young man,' said Matron Bright. 'We think it is too.'

'Hello Matron Bright,' Alice-Miranda greeted the woman.

Marigold wriggled a little dance then wrapped her arms around the child and hugged her tightly. 'Hello, my lovely girl, what a wonderful surprise to have you in the first group. It's such a pleasure to see you. It's been far too long.'

'That's because I've been so busy at school,' Alice-Miranda announced. 'I can't wait to see everyone and I could hardly believe my eyes when Mummy and Daddy pulled up outside – and best of all, Uncle Ed is with them too.'

'Excellent,' said Matron Bright. 'We'll get everyone sorted here and then I'll go and find them.'

'Are they just visiting for the day?' Alice-Miranda asked the woman.

'Didn't they tell you? Your uncle has come to sort through your grandmother's art collection. He's doing a very important job. He's going to be staying with us for the next week at least. Perhaps longer.'

Alice-Miranda jumped up and down and clapped her hands. 'I'll be able to see him every day!'

Caprice was watching Alice-Miranda. The child was ridiculous and that woman, Matron Bright – did anyone ever really smile that much?

'Come along, everyone,' Matron Bright instructed. 'We've got some people in the reading room who are very excited to meet you.'

Chapter 17

Soon enough the ten Barn Owls had been assigned their jobs for the morning.

'Do you want to swap?' Jacinta whispered to Alice-Miranda. 'Sloane and I have to go and read to some dribbly oldies in the nursing home wing. What if they don't have any teeth?'

Alice-Miranda grinned. 'You'll be fine. Just check the water glasses next to the bed before you take a drink.'

'What for?' Jacinta asked.

'Their teeth,' Alice-Miranda giggled.

Jacinta shuddered. 'Eww, gross!'

'I'm joking,' said Alice-Miranda.

Figgy had been matched with Mr Mobbs and Rufus was spending the morning with Mr Johnson.

Mr Mobbs was less than impressed with the pairing and began sniffing the air as soon as Figgy sat beside him. 'Did you use deodorant this morning, son?'

Figgy nodded, wondering what the old bloke was getting at.

'Well, you need some more. I told you children smell, matron. This one here is right on the nose.' The old man pinched his nostrils and pulled a face.

Millie had been assigned to Mrs Von Thripp and Alice-Miranda was going to chat with Mr Freeman.

'I wonder if he's related to that detective we met yesterday?' Alice-Miranda said to Millie.

'Hopefully he's not as grumpy as she was,' Millie replied.

Caprice, Susannah, Lucas and Sep were off to join the gardening team. That revelation hadn't sat well with Jacinta, who had caught Lucas staring at Caprice that morning at breakfast. Then again, he wasn't the only one.

'Hello Mr Freeman,' said Alice-Miranda as she approached the old man. She remembered his face from some of her earlier visits. 'My name is Alice-Miranda Highton-Smith-Kennington-Jones.' She held out her hand.

Donald smiled at her. 'Are you Cecelia's little girl? You've grown up a bit since the last time you were here.'

'Oh, yes. I've started boarding school. I love it. I have lots of friends and we get to do loads of interesting things, but that means I don't have a lot of time to visit any more,' Alice-Miranda replied.

Donald nodded.

'Yesterday we met a detective whose last name was Freeman,' the child said. 'Do you know her?'

'That's my daughter,' Donald replied.

'We were on a bus and there was a silly mix-up,' Alice-Miranda explained. 'I don't think she was very happy about it.'

'No, but she's not very happy about a lot of things,' Donald said with a sigh.

Alice-Miranda rummaged inside her day pack for a pen and the question sheet that Mr Plumpton had supplied. She scanned the page. 'How long have you lived at Pelham Park?'

'I came here not long after the renovations were completed. That was about seven years ago now, I think,' Mr Freeman replied.

'What do you enjoy about living here?'

'My apartment is lovely and there are lots of people to keep a fellow company in his old age. Oh and Matron Bright – she's a delight.'

Alice-Miranda nodded. 'Have you lived on the estate before?'

Donald looked at the child closely.

Alice-Miranda thought his eyes were the loveliest colour, like sea water – not quite green and not blue either.

'Did you work here?' Alice-Miranda prompted.

Donald shook his head. 'No. I grew up here.'

'Oh really? That must have been interesting. Was it a terribly long time ago? I'm sorry but it would be rude of me to guess your age,' Alice-Miranda prattled.

'I'm almost eighty-five,' Donald replied. 'And yes, it was a very long time ago. Until I was fifteen, so that's . . .'

Alice-Miranda did the numbers in her head. 'Seventy years. That does seem a long time. Do you remember it well?'

Donald closed his eyes. A smile perched on his lips as if a clear memory had just come into view. 'Like it was yesterday. We lived over the rise in one of the cottages. My father was a butler in the house.'

'You must have had lots of friends to play with,' said Alice-Miranda.

She watched the man. His hands trembled a little and a roadmap of green veins tracked underneath his thinning skin.

'Yes.'

'Was there anyone you remember?' she asked.

'Harry. He was my best friend,' Donald said. His eyes sprung open. He must have been getting soft in his old age. He hadn't spoken of Harry in years. He didn't deserve to occupy Donald's thoughts. Not after what he did.

'How lovely to have such a good friend. Did you know my grandpa at all?' Alice-Miranda asked, wide-eyed. She wondered if the two men would have been a similar age.

Donald shrugged. 'A bit.' His face took on a steely expression.

'What was he like? I don't know much about him at all, except that he wasn't very kind to Daddy and Uncle Ed when they were growing up, and Granny Arabella died and it broke his heart.'

'I don't remember,' Donald snapped. 'We left when I was fifteen.'

'But, surely if you knew him you must remember something,' Alice-Miranda pleaded. 'Was he happy as a boy?'

'I told you. I don't know.' Donald shook his head.

Alice-Miranda had a feeling there was something Mr Freeman wasn't telling her. 'Why did you leave?'

'We just did,' Donald answered abruptly and pulled at his collar. 'Is it warm in here?'

'No, I don't think so. I was actually going to put my jacket on,' Alice-Miranda replied as she looked around for the offending draught.

Matron Bright reappeared. 'Time's almost up I'm afraid, but you can continue tomorrow,' she announced. 'I trust you all had a lovely meeting.'

'Goodbye, Mr Freeman. See you again soon,' said Alice-Miranda. She was wondering if she would see her parents and uncle before heading back to Bagley Hall.

But the old man didn't reply. He was staring off into the distance.

'Did you enjoy yourselves?' Mr Plumpton asked as he rejoined the group in the Great Hall. Beth had returned to the camp to set up their afternoon activities.

'Mr Mobbs said I smelled,' Figgy scoffed.

Rufus sniffed the air. 'You do.'

'Not as bad as him. You should have seen the blanket on his knees fluttering up and down and then his eyebrows would get all pointy and he'd look at me as if I'd done it.'

The children laughed.

'Alice-Miranda, your parents asked if they could see you for a minute before we head back over to camp,' said Mr Plumpton. 'I believe they're in the office.'

'I'll take you,' Matron Bright offered.

'We'll be in the garden. Beth is coming back to walk over with us, and we won't go without you,' the teacher said.

'Thanks, Mr Plumpton,' Alice-Miranda said. 'Can Millie come with me? I know Mummy and Daddy would love to see her too.'

'No, Millie can stay with us this time,' Mr Plumpton decided.

Millie's face fell. Clearly Mr Plumpton didn't trust her at the moment. She hated that the teachers believed she'd pushed Caprice in the pool.

'Sorry,' Alice-Miranda mouthed.

'Come along, dear.' Matron Bright bounced away with Alice-Miranda beside her.

Chapter 18

'There you are, darling.' Cecelia Highton-Smith stood up as Alice-Miranda and Matron Bright appeared at the office door. 'I was just going to come and find you.'

'We have to go back to camp in a minute,' the child said.

A beeper went off in the matron's pocket. She pulled it out and popped her glasses on the tip of her nose. 'Oh, excuse me. That's Mr Mobbs again. He's probably ordered something from the television that he wants me to pick up from the post office.' The woman chortled. 'He really can't help himself.'

'See you tomorrow, matron,' Alice-Miranda said.

'Yes, dear, see you tomorrow.' Marigold gave a wave and bounded away.

'So, did you had fun with your oldie?' her father asked with a wink.

'Yes, Daddy.' Alice-Miranda's eyes twinkled. 'Mr Freeman is lovely. He lived here on the estate when he was a little boy but he said that his family left when he was fifteen. He wouldn't tell me any more. His daughter's a detective. We met her yesterday when she pulled the minibus over.'

'What was that, darling?' Cecelia gasped.

'It's all right, Mummy. The bus had been stolen –' Alice-Miranda began.

'Stolen! This just gets better and better.' Cecelia shook her head.

'No, Mummy. It wasn't stolen any more. It had been returned but the detective didn't know that and so it was just a silly mix-up.'

Ed Clifton frowned. 'Freeman. Freeman . . . That name rings a bell.'

'He's very old, Uncle Ed. Much older than you, of course. I think he knew Grandpa when they were boys,' Alice-Miranda said. 'But when I asked him what Grandpa was like, he said he couldn't remember and he got a bit cross.'

'Oh, Freeman's probably quite a common name,' said Ed.

'Matron Bright said that you're going to sort out Granny's art collection,' Alice-Miranda told her uncle.

Ed nodded.

'Your uncle has a huge job ahead of him. I should have taken care of it years ago, but it's worked out far better to have Ed do it,' Hugh said.

'Where is it?' Alice-Miranda asked.

'Downstairs in a vault in the cellars. We were just checking in here for any paperwork,' Hugh explained. 'It's a pity you have to go back to camp. Perhaps I could ask Mr Plumpton if you can stay? Ed could walk you back later.'

Alice-Miranda shook her head. 'Sorry, Daddy. We have rock climbing straight after lunch and, besides, I wouldn't want anyone to think that I was getting special privileges. We're here again tomorrow – maybe Uncle Ed could take me to have a look then.'

'That sounds like a good idea,' Cecelia agreed.

Alice-Miranda said goodbye to her parents and uncle and skipped off to join her friends at the front of the house.

Meanwhile, outside, Caprice was at work.

'Mr Plumpton, do we have to have partners for rock climbing?' she asked.

'I presume you will,' the man replied.

'If we do, can we swap partners from yesterday so that everyone has to learn to rely on everyone else?' she said sweetly.

Mr Plumpton looked at the girl. 'That sounds like a very good idea, Caprice.'

A smile spread across her face. 'I'd like to have Millie as my partner to show her that there are no hard feelings about what she did to me at the pool yesterday.'

'Caprice, that is very gracious of you,' the teacher said. 'What a mature thing to ask.'

Millie's stomach knotted. She wondered what Caprice was up to this time. Once Caprice had turned away, she walked over to the teacher.

'Mr Plumpton, I – I don't know if that's such a good idea,' Millie whispered.

'Millie,' the teacher admonished, 'Caprice has offered you the hand of friendship. I'm surprised at you.'

Caprice came and stood beside the girl. 'Come on, Millie. Rock climbing will be fun. I've done it before so I know how everything works.'

Millie gulped. That was exactly what she was afraid of.

Alice-Miranda rushed down the front steps and rejoined the group.

'Sorry, Ed, but Cee and I have to get going. I've got some meetings out of town but I'll be home tomorrow night and Cee will be back for the anniversary fair on Saturday,' Hugh Kennington-Jones apologised and glanced at his watch. 'I wish we could stay to show you around.'

'Where are you off to?' Ed asked.

'I'm going to a farm to look at their organic vegetable-growing processes and Cee's off to a health retreat with one of her girlfriends. I think I dodged a bullet with that one. Don't fancy kale and watercress soup, do you?'

'Nope,' Ed grinned.

'I heard that.' Cecelia looked up from the far desk, where she was checking arrangements for the fair. 'I'm sure my trip will be very . . . refreshing.'

'That's one word for it,' Hugh said, a cheeky glint in his eye. 'Anyway, Ed, I'm not sure how my phone reception will be – last time I was there it was pretty hit and miss, and Cee's break is a "no technology" affair. If you need anything just call Dolly and she'll be able to get in touch with one of us.'

'I'll be fine, Hugh. It will be great to have time to go through things,' Ed said.

'Come on, darling, we'd better get moving,' Hugh called to Cecelia.

Ed stood on the front steps and waved as his brother and sister-in-law drove away. Thin wisps of clouds fanned out across a dazzling sapphire sky. Ed wished he'd brought his paints with him – the light was magnificent.

'Well, old man, it's time to lay some ghosts to rest,' Ed whispered.

Chapter 19

Lunchtime in the dining room was a noisy affair, with the children competing to tell the most exciting stories from their activities so far.

Danika and Shelby stopped by to chat with Alice-Miranda and her friends about the climbing wall, which they said was terrifying and thrilling at the same time, while Sloane spilled far too many beans about the treasure hunt.

'I am never going to complain about anything Mrs Smith makes ever again,' said Jacinta.

She prodded the soggy cheese nachos in front of her.

'It's not too bad,' Alice-Miranda said, 'if you eat it quickly.'

'Ugh, yuck,' Caprice whined as she hopped up from the table to scrape her plate. She headed outside to the toilet.

On her way back, she spotted Mr Plumpton and Miss Reedy. The pair were standing outside the teacher's lounge, talking quietly. Caprice walked around the side of the building, taking care to stay out of sight. She was keen to get some proof of their love affair.

'So, who do you think will win the Queen's Medal?' Mr Plumpton asked.

Caprice's ears pricked up. This was far better than some lovey-dovey chitchat.

'It's early days, but if I was a betting woman I'd put the house on Alice-Miranda. She's incredibly resourceful and an excellent problem-solver.' Miss Reedy checked her watch and sighed. 'We should get back inside.'

Caprice's blood felt like lava and her eardrums began to throb. She shot off back to the dining room, and missed Mr Plumpton's reply.

'I don't know, Livinia. Alice-Miranda is in with a very good chance, but I've been terribly impressed with Sep Sykes. Caprice is an interesting one too.'

Back inside, Alice-Miranda was thinking about their next activity.

'Are you really okay about being Caprice's partner for the climbing wall?' she whispered to Millie.

'I don't have a choice,' Millie said.

'I'll watch her.' Alice-Miranda reached over and gave Millie's arm a squeeze.

Just as the groups were getting ready to go, Miss Wall wheeled a large whiteboard into the dining room. It had the names of all the groups down one side and the days marked at the top. Miss Reedy walked to the small podium at the end of the room and switched on the microphone.

'How exciting, Miss Wall. I see we have our first group points to reveal. Have you got the list?'

Benitha Wall smiled. 'Sure have.'

The children craned their necks to see the scores as the PE teacher wrote them neatly in the first column.

'How can the Robins have more points than the Barn Owls?' Caprice huffed. 'They're babies.'

'We'll just have to try harder,' Alice-Miranda said.

The scores for all thirteen teams were on the board. The Robins had done well but the Ospreys were leading the way.

The group cheered loudly when Miss Reedy announced the result.

'Danika, come and get your team's prize,' Miss Reedy directed, 'and don't eat them all at once.' She handed the girl a bag of chocolate frogs.

'Don't worry, the teachers will rig it anyway,' Jacinta said. 'I bet every group wins something.'

'You're such a cynic,' Sloane replied. 'But you're probably right.'

'All right, everyone. Calm down. There's one other thing I'd like to mention before you head off to your next activities. As you are aware, a special medal will be presented by Queen Georgiana herself to the student who impresses us most while working towards their Blue. I thought it might be interesting to let you know the names of some children who have already come to our attention. This might spur some others to put in a little more effort.' The woman glared in Figgy's direction. 'Congratulations to Danika, Ivory, Sep, Alice-Miranda and Caprice. I hope to see the rest of you aspiring to similar levels of achievement. And remember, it's not just about completing the tasks, it's about the spirit with which you do it and the way you work with others to get there. Off you go, everyone. Have a lovely afternoon.'

Millie couldn't believe her ears. She glanced at Caprice, expecting her to look like the cat who got the cream, but the girl's pretty face was stony.

Caprice's mind was racing. It sounded as if the teachers had already decided who was going to win the Queen's Medal. Not if she had anything to do with it. Caprice stared into space as a plot began to hatch.

The children stood up and deposited their plates on the servery, grabbed a piece of fruit and filled their water bottles, then went to meet their camp leaders at the back doors.

'Is everyone here?' Beth counted the heads. 'Okay, who's ready to climb?'

A cheer went up from the group.

Beth and Mr Plumpton led the children to a four-sided tower in the middle of the camp. Each wall was covered with coloured hand- and footholds, and had a varying degree of difficulty. Beth introduced the children to the climbing instructor, Warren.

'Hi there.' Warren smiled at the children. He was a broad-shouldered young man with sandy blond curls and muscly arms that bore several colourful tattoos.

'Cool ink,' Figgy said.

Warren grinned at the boy. 'Thanks.'

'What would you know about tattoos?' Jacinta said.

'I'm going to get one as soon as I'm old enough,' Figgy said.

'What of?' Sloane asked.

'I was thinking about a dragon with a tail that whips around my middle.' Figgy ran his hand from back to front under his rib cage.

'Sounds disgusting,' Jacinta said, screwing up her nose. 'I don't like tattoos at all. My granny has one. It started out as a butterfly but now that everything's gone south, it looks like a bat.'

Everyone laughed.

'Thanks, I'll keep that in mind before I get any more,' Warren said. 'Now, I need a volunteer to show how you fit your harnesses properly.'

A forest of arms shot into the air.

Warren glanced at Mr Plumpton.

'Oh no, no, no, don't look at me.' The teacher waved his hands like little windscreen wipers.

'But if the teachers are too scared to have a go, how can we expect the students to get up there?' Warren said slowly. It seemed he knew every trick in the book.

'Go on, Mr P,' Rufus shouted.

'You can do it, Mr Plumpton,' Sloane called.

Figgy started a chant: 'Mr P' followed by three claps. It took seconds for the rest of the group to join in, including Beth and Warren.

Josiah Plumpton's cheeks flushed red. 'Oh, all right. I can only give it a try.' His stomach did a little backflip as he looked up at the wall, which soared fifteen metres into the sky.

Warren fitted a blue helmet on Mr Plumpton's head, showing the children how to tighten the strap. He knocked his fist on the top three times to show how well it protected Mr Plumpton's skull.

'Steady on there,' Mr Plumpton complained. 'You'll give me a concussion.'

Warren then pulled out a red harness. 'Now, step through here.' He nodded at the first leg hole. 'And now through here.'

Mr Plumpton put one leg in at a time and Warren helped pull the webbed straps up around the teacher's bottom, showing the children how to secure each of the fastenings.

'It has to be tight,' the instructor said. 'You shouldn't be able to get more than one finger through the gap.'

Mr Plumpton gasped as the young instructor pulled the straps and tucked them away.

'Hey, sir, you've got a giant wedgie,' Figgy called.

The group laughed.

Warren spun Mr Plumpton around and showed the children where they would attach the clip to the front. He held up the metal fastener. 'Does anyone know what this is called?'

'It's a carabiner,' said Caprice.

Warren grinned. 'You're right. This is a critical piece of equipment, so it's important that you don't drop it or damage it. If you do, you have to tell me.'

The young man snapped a carabiner onto the front of Mr Plumpton's harness and pulled out a rope that was dangling from the wall. He attached it to the carabiner.

'The reason you have to work in pairs is that everyone must have someone below, holding the ropes. It's called belaying and it's the most important job of all. We don't want anyone falling.'

Millie gulped. She wondered if that's what Caprice was playing at. Was she going to wait until she reached the top then drop her like a rock?

Caprice leaned towards her. 'Don't look so worried, Millie. You'll be fine up there. You'd better look after me too.'

Millie shivered.

'Are you ready, Mr Plumpton?' Warren looked at the man, who was completely kitted out and attached to the ropes.

The teacher shook his head. 'No, no, no. I was just demonstrating how to put the equipment on. You don't really think I'm going up there,?

'Yes, you are,' Warren said forcefully.

'Oh dear. I've never done this before.' He might as well have been scaling Mount Everest for the way he was feeling. 'I'm a Science teacher. I know about gravity.'

'Just get as far as you can. And don't worry. I've got you. You won't fall,' Warren reassured him.

'Go on, Mr P . . . you can do it,' the children chorused as the teacher took his first wobbly step onto the lowest foothold.

Mr Plumpton propelled himself forward and reached up with his right hand, grabbing a red hold. Before too long he was several metres off the ground.

He wasn't aware that Livinia Reedy was now watching too. She'd been on her way to check on the group in the swimming pool when she spotted Mr Plumpton halfway up the wall. Her heart was pounding as the squat little man hauled himself higher and higher. Josiah was no athlete but she was terribly proud to see him taking on the challenge.

'You're almost there, sir,' Figgy cried out.

Josiah could see the top of the frame but his legs were burning and perspiration poured from his brow. 'I don't think I can go any further,' he wheezed.

Harold Lipp had just joined the group too. He'd been annoyed when his lunch was interrupted by a call to bring a first-aid kit to the archery range. The group should have taken it with them, of course, but in the excitement had left it behind. Mr Trout had made it sound as if he had a hole in his hand but when Mr Lipp got there with the medical supplies it turned out to be barely a scratch. Honestly, he thought, some of the teachers were bigger drama queens than the students.

'What's Plumpton doing up there?' he hissed at Miss Reedy, who was startled by his stealthy approach.

'Being a fine role model,' she replied.

'Don't look down, sir,' Figgy shouted.

Of course that was the very first thing the teacher did. He was surprised to see Mr Lipp and Miss Reedy watching him.

'All right, Plumpy, you've had your fun. Obviously you can't get to the top so come down and give the children a turn, will you? They're the ones endeavouring to earn an award,' Mr Lipp yelled.

'Come on, Mr P, don't give up,' Rufus called. 'You're almost there.'

'Yeah, sir, show Mr Lipp what you're made of,' Lucas urged the teacher.

Livinia Reedy looked on proudly and gave two thumbs up. It was all he needed and from somewhere, Mr Plumpton managed to drag himself to the top, where he banged his hand against the metal frame three times.

'Woohoo!' Mr Plumpton shouted. He pumped his fist in the air.

'Wonderful, Josiah, just wonderful,' said Miss Reedy. She had a tear in her eye.

'Hurry up then, Plumpton. Down you come. I'm sure the children don't care about seeing you up there all afternoon,' Mr Lipp scoffed.

'You should have a go, Mr Lipp,' Sep Sykes suggested.

Mr Lipp stormed away.

Mr Plumpton dangled at the top of the wall like a human plumb-bob as Warren slowly lowered him back down.

To everyone's surprise, Miss Reedy rushed forward and gave the man a hug.

'Miss Reedy, what are you doing?' Mr Plumpton whispered as his nose lit up.

The woman leapt back as if she'd been bitten by a cobra. 'Oh, I don't know what came over me.' She smoothed her pants and fixed her hair. 'I was just so relieved to see you safely back down again, Mr Plumpton. Job well done.' And with that the teacher turned and scurried away.

'They're so cute,' Jacinta said. 'I hope they get married.'

Mr Plumpton removed his harness and helmet and slunk away to get a drink and cool down. He hoped he might stop shaking too.

Minutes later the children were harnessed, helmeted and climbing.

Jacinta practically ran to the top. It was like watching a spider monkey.

'Still want to race me, Figgy?' she shouted down to the boy, who was realising that it was harder than it looked.

He shook his head.

Alice-Miranda teamed up with Lucas and both made it to the top.

Millie waited while Caprice climbed first. Yet again the girl was a superstar, almost as agile as Jacinta. Millie wondered if there was anything she couldn't do.

'Are you ready?' Caprice asked Millie. Mr Plumpton was standing right beside them.

'You're not . . . you're not going to do anything, are you?' Millie squeaked. Her face was ashen and she was shaking.

'Really?' Caprice asked. 'How could you even think that? I told you there were no hard feelings.'

But Millie didn't believe her. Why would she say there were no hard feelings when it was Caprice who had set up the whole incident at the pool? She'd threatened Millie, and Millie was the one who'd got in trouble for it. But today she was as nice as pie.

Alice-Miranda leapt down from the wall and unclipped her harness. She walked over and stood right behind Caprice.

'Go on, Millie,' Alice-Miranda encouraged her friend.

Millie began tentatively. She pushed up, making sure that the rope was tight each time she progressed.

Caprice was doing everything right as far as Alice-Miranda could tell. She fed the rope through and strained on it when she needed to. Maybe she really was sorry for what she'd done the day before.

After what seemed like an age, Millie reached the top and banged on the frame.

'Well done, Millie,' Alice-Miranda shouted, and the other children waiting below gave a cheer.

As Millie dangled from the top, Alice-Miranda watched Caprice lower Millie steadily until the girl's feet hit the ground.

Millie beamed and let out a huge sigh of relief. Alice-Miranda rushed forward and gave her a hug.

'How was that, Millie?' Mr Plumpton asked.

'Good.' She was still shaking but relieved to have got up and down in one piece.

'See, told you everything would be fine,' Caprice said with a smile.

'Oh, I'm so pleased that you two are getting along,' Mr Plumpton said happily. 'Well done,

Caprice. Well done, Millie.' He was scribbling something on the page on his clipboard.

Alice-Miranda was relieved too. But something still didn't feel right. Caprice had just done everything by the book yet Alice-Miranda couldn't shake that niggling feeling that this wasn't the end of her dispute with Millie. Caprice was complicated: brilliant, beautiful and, if everything Millie had told her was true, quite possibly the most conniving person Alice-Miranda had ever met – which was saying something.

'Come on, Millie, do you want to get a drink?' Caprice asked.

Millie looked at Alice-Miranda.

'Go on,' she mouthed and gave a small nod.

The girls rushed over to where their day packs were lined up along the fence.

Chapter 20

Ed Clifton had walked for miles through the estate village, whose cottages were now inhabited by the staff who looked after the residents of Pelham Park; past the farmhouses and the lake and the river where he had learned to fish as a boy; and through the woodlands, which to his great joy were still exactly as he'd remembered.

He reflected fondly on school holidays spent roaming around with the estate children whose lives he would gladly have traded places with in a blink.

They'd always thought him so lucky to live in the big house with all those people to look after him. But for Ed it had been like growing up in a straitjacket. He could recall a few family picnics but they were always grand affairs with servants on hand and guests who had come from all over the world – usually people associated with his father's work. Nothing was ever done just for fun.

Ed decided he'd seen enough for one day. He glanced at the hilltop. On top was the family vault, its stark cross standing out against the blue sky. He would visit them soon. Just not yet. He had been glad to hear that his brother had removed his own memorial as soon as the two of them were reunited. Seeing it would have been strange, to say the least. Then again, in some peculiar way he did bury Xavier Kennington-Jones when he left home and became Ed Clifton all those years ago.

Ed walked into the house and almost bumped into Matron Bright.

'Good afternoon, Mr Clifton,' she said with a smile. 'I trust you had an enjoyable walk.'

'Yes thank you, matron. I should like to make a start downstairs. Will I need any keys to get to the cellar?'

'Oh yes, of course. I'll get you a set now. I'm afraid I keep everything locked up tight. I had a set go missing when we first opened – never found them and it's always worried me. I'd hate for any of our residents to go wandering and find themselves somewhere they're not familiar with.' She darted away and soon returned with the keys.

Ed walked along the hallway to the rear stairs. He knew his way to the cellars, having spent a great deal of time down there with his paints. Ed was just twelve years old when, with his mother's help, he'd set up a studio at the far end of the subterranean maze. The light was terrible but he'd been able to toil away during term breaks without fear of his father finding out. Initially he had attempted to copy the works of artists he admired, before beginning to find his own unique style.

One evening, when Ed was away at university and about to take his final examinations, his father had gone in search of some long-lost object that he'd decided must be in the cellars. When Henry discovered Ed's secret he was furious. No son of his was going to be an artist – not when there was a company to run and a legacy to continue.

Henry Kennington-Jones destroyed every canvas and had the studio dismantled. No amount of pleading from his wife would make Henry see sense – he hadn't stopped to discover that Ed's work wasn't just good, it was incredible. It wasn't until Ed returned home at the end of semester that he discovered everything was gone. He'd felt as if the air had been sucked out of his lungs.

When Ed had confronted his father, there was a terrible row. They'd fought before but never like this. A week later, Ed had packed his things and left for the United States to pursue his dreams. The very next night his mother was gone too.

Ed's chest tightened as he walked downstairs. He felt like a boy again.

He turned the key in the lock and pushed open the door at the end of the butler's pantry, careful to lock it behind him as Matron Bright had requested. Ed flicked the switch and a dull glow lit the stairs. The air was immediately cooler. He knew from experience that so long as moisture hadn't penetrated the walls, the cellar's constant temperature made it almost the perfect place to store artwork.

He reached the bottom and unlocked the second door. His hand reached instinctively for the light switch.

The cellars had always contained household cast-offs but he was stunned by just how much more had migrated downstairs. Strewn among the sideboards, lamps and other furniture, his grandfather's and father's collection of ghastly trophies were unmissable – although Ed did have a soft spot for Sidney, the polar bear who used to live in his father's study.

'How's things?' He looked up at the giant beast with its yellowing fur.

Ed picked a path between the goods, wondering how much anyone really needed in life.

He had always known about the vault. It was like an old-fashioned panic room, but he had never been allowed to see it as a boy. He pulled aside a black curtain and faced the vault door. Hugh had told him the combination of the lock – it wasn't hard to remember, as it was the year Pelham Park was founded. Now two of them knew that secret. Ed turned the dial and pulled on the weighty metal handle. Instead of another jumble, he was surprised to find a vast, well-organised space with a large set of storage racks.

Ed walked among the canvases, marvelling at the sheer number and realising just what a big job lay ahead of him.

'Oh my goodness,' he said as he caught sight of a still life his mother had loved. She'd had it moved to hang in his bedroom after he'd commented on the light and shade. He was fairly certain it was a Caravaggio.

There were pencil sketches, oils, reliefs and a small selection of modern art among the more traditional portraits, still lifes and landscapes. Hugh had been right to seek his help. It would take days to go through properly. The collection would bring a pretty penny at auction, although Hugh had mentioned that Ed should think about what he would like for himself too.

Ed's mind raced as he struggled to remember which pieces had been displayed in the house. He smiled to himself. He and his mother had often conversed about the origins of the works and their style. It was a love they shared.

Ed reached into his pocket. He wondered if his phone would pick up a signal down there, as he wanted to catch Hugh before his trip.

He looked at the screen and saw a single bar, but as the telephone rang it went straight to messages.

'Hugh, Ed here,' he said. 'I'm downstairs at the moment and this is amazing. I don't think I realised what an astute collector Mother was. There are works she bought from young artists that will be worth a considerable amount now as well as some incredible old stuff too.'

As he was leaving the message, something caught Ed's eye. 'Anyway, I'll start on making a list and then we can get someone in to take a look at it all in a few days. Have a good trip.'

Ed walked towards the furthest rack. A large landscape jutted out from behind a portrait of a beautiful woman.

Ed put his phone back into his trouser pocket and pulled the landscape out, studying it closely.

'No,' he gasped. 'It's not possible.'

He peered at the bottom right-hand corner. Even in the dim light, he knew what he was looking at. The signature just confirmed it. Monet.

'I don't remember this being here.' Ed swallowed hard. He knew that it couldn't be there. It shouldn't be there. And he knew that because he was almost certain the painting was stolen.

Chapter 21

After rock climbing, the Barn Owls had a short break before they went to archery. Mr Plumpton mapped out a boundary and gave strict instructions that the children could play some ball games but there was to be no use of other camp equipment. He was dying for a cup of tea and thought that the children could be trusted on their own for a few minutes.

Everyone seemed happy to find a shady spot and have a rest.

'Who do you think was the fastest up the wall?' Sloane asked.

'That's easy, it was Jacinta,' said Lucas. He smiled at the girl, who'd just sat down beside him.

Jacinta's heart skipped a beat.

Caprice's pretty eyes turned dark.

'I don't know,' Sep said. 'Caprice was pretty speedy. I think it would have been close if the girls had a race.'

Caprice's thunderous look disappeared as she flicked her ponytail and smiled at the boy.

'Thanks, Sep,' she said.

Alice-Miranda watched the girl closely. She wondered what was going on in that head of hers and if she really was sorry about what had happened the afternoon before with Millie.

Beth approached them from the teacher's lounge. Mr Plumpton, balancing a cup of tea and biscuit, followed behind her.

'Hey everyone, let's get going. Hope you're all keen to shoot some targets,' Beth called.

Caprice smiled. She had one in mind.

The archery range was only a short walk away on the edge of the woods, past the high-ropes course. Soon they sat in front of four targets, waiting to begin.

'I need a volunteer,' Beth said.

Josiah Plumpton firmly shook his head. He wasn't giving up his cup of tea for anyone.

The young woman pointed. 'Caprice.'

Caprice was kitted out with an arm guard and a large bow. Beth stood behind her, demonstrating how to draw the string back and release it.

'May I shoot an arrow, please?' Caprice asked sweetly.

'Sure,' Beth said. 'Before we start, I need you to make sure that you *always* point your arrows towards the targets. And it doesn't matter if you run out, you're not to go and retrieve them until I've called "all clear" and *all* bows are on the ground. Is that understood?'

The children nodded.

Beth handed Caprice an arrow. The girl fumbled about for a few seconds, trying to get it to stay in the nocking point, which held it steady on the string.

Caprice grinned. 'It's harder than it looks.'

Beth nodded. 'You're right about that. But don't worry. No one expects you to be an expert first time.'

Caprice steadied herself and pulled back the string.

Millie was watching closely. Caprice's fumbling fingers transformed almost instantaneously and suddenly the girl looked as if she knew exactly what she was doing.

Caprice released the arrow. It flew through the air and landed in the centre ring of the yellow bullseye.

A huge cheer erupted from the group.

Beth looked at the girl quizzically. 'So you've just picked up a bow for the first time, then?'

'Maybe?' Caprice shrugged, not prepared to give anything away. She took another arrow from the quiver slung across her shoulder and lined it up.

It sliced through the air and again hit the target, lodging right beside the first arrow.

'Whoa! You're amazing!' Sep called.

Three more arrows found the target, although one ended up slightly off centre in the red ring.

'Caprice, that was remarkable.' Mr Plumpton gave the girl a clap. 'Well done, my dear.'

After Caprice had finished showing off her extraordinary skills, the children spread out and lined up at the four targets.

Beth and Mr Plumpton watched and helped where they could.

No matter how hard Susannah tried, she simply couldn't get the arrow to fly further than a few feet. Figgy managed to hit the target twice, while Sep and Rufus did even better, although no one came close to Caprice's impressive feat.

Beth raised her hand in the air once the four shooters' quivers were spent. 'Bows down. Now off you go and get the arrows.'

Susannah didn't have to go far to retrieve hers and returned quickly to put them into Millie's quiver. Soon the next group was lined up ready to try their luck.

Millie was on the end, with Alice-Miranda next, then Lucas and Jacinta. The children were given the all clear to take their first shots.

Just as Millie raised the bow and pulled the string back, Caprice shouted. 'Millie! Watch out!'

Millie spun around and ducked, but before she realised what she was doing she'd released the arrow. It skimmed along the ground past Alice-Miranda's, Lucas's and Jacinta's feet and stopped just shy of Mr Plumpton's boots.

Beth flew over to the girl and yanked the bow out of her hand. Millie's face was ashen.

'I'm . . . I'm . . . so sorry,' she said, trembling. 'I didn't mean to . . .'

'What were you thinking, Millie?' Beth demanded. 'You could have killed someone.'

'But Caprice yelled at me to watch out and I didn't realise I would shoot.' Millie's eyes filled with tears.

'There was a wasp,' Caprice said. 'It was huge and I thought she was going to be stung.'

Alice-Miranda put her bow on the ground and raced over to comfort her friend. 'It's all right. Nobody was hurt.'

'That arrow – it went right past you,' Millie sniffed.

'That's right. It went *past* me,' said Alice-Miranda. 'I'm still here.'

Beth and Mr Plumpton were standing to the side of the group, deep in conversation.

'Millie, could you come here, please?' the Science teacher requested.

She walked over to the pair.

'We think you'd better sit the rest of the archery out,' the teacher informed her. 'I'm afraid you won't be receiving a pass for this activity.'

Millie nodded. Her hands were shaking so much she wouldn't have been able to hit anything anyway. 'I'm so sorry,' she whispered.

‘We know you are. But you simply have to be more careful,’ Mr Plumpton said.

‘Caprice startled me.’ Millie had begun to calm down enough to realise that the whole thing wouldn’t have happened if Caprice hadn’t called out.

‘She was only trying to stop you from being stung.’ Right on cue a huge wasp began to buzz around Mr Plumpton’s head. He ducked and wove to avoid the cranky creature.

Millie had been wondering if there was a wasp at all. She walked back to a seat on the rise behind the shooters and sat down, tears still trickling.

Caprice walked over to join her. ‘That was bad luck. But at least you didn’t get stung.’

‘If there really was a wasp,’ Millie snapped.

‘What? You don’t believe me?’ Caprice said. ‘Silly you.’

‘Just leave me alone,’ Millie said.

‘No,’ Caprice snarled. ‘You’re going to help me.’

Millie wondered what she was getting at. The last thing she wanted to do was help Caprice.

‘I don’t like to lose, Millie. I think you know that now. I’m going to win the Queen’s medal,’ Caprice informed her.

'You might. But you're not the only one in the running.' Millie wiped her face and looked at the girl defiantly.

'No, it seems that I'm not. But that's where you come in. You see, I don't like your little friend Alice-Miranda very much. I don't like anyone here, but you've proved useful,' Caprice explained.

'I'm not helping you with anything. I knew it was all an act, you being so careful at rock climbing. And just now I could have impaled someone or worse. You did it on purpose, didn't you?' Millie tugged at her collar and rubbed her neck. She could feel a prickly heat rash coming on.

Caprice smirked. 'Think what you like, but you will help me. Because you know what I'm capable of.'

'You're nuts!' Millie shook her head. 'As if I'm not going to tell the teachers what you're up to.'

'I don't think you will. If you do, I can't guarantee that the next time your little friend gets that close to an arrow it won't be . . . messy. There are still plenty more dangerous activities to do before we go home. And if you want her to stay in one piece, then I suggest you do everything I say from now on.'

'You're bluffing. You wouldn't really hurt her,' Millie said.

'Want to know why I left my last school?' Caprice arched her eyebrow menacingly.

Millie gulped. She wasn't sure that she did.

'There was a horrible accident and one of the girls fell down a flight of stairs,' Caprice said.

Millie gasped. 'Did you push her?'

Caprice narrowed her eyes. 'You'll never know.'

'If you win the stupid medal, will you leave me alone?' Millie asked.

'Of course.' Caprice smirked again. 'Maybe we could even be friends.'

Millie felt as if she might throw up. She would never be friends with Caprice. 'Fine then. Just tell me what I have to do.'

Millie didn't want to believe that Caprice was really capable of hurting anyone. But she couldn't know for sure. And there was no way she was going to test the theory on her best friend.

Hugh Kennington-Jones telephoned his brother as soon as his meeting finished.

'Hi Ed, did you find it all?' Hugh asked.

'More than I imagined,' Ed replied.

'Oh really? That sounds promising. Do you think we'll be able to add some funds to the trust?' Hugh enquired.

Ed laughed. 'Put it this way, I don't think you'll have to worry about Pelham Park's financial security again.'

'Brilliant!' Hugh said.

A loud whumping sound began to drown out their conversation.

'Hugh, we need to talk about something I found,' Ed began. He could barely hear himself speak.

'Sorry Ed, I've got to get going.' Hugh could see his wife sitting in the back of the chopper, tapping her watch.

'But it's important, Hugh.' Ed realised he was yelling.

'Sorry, I can't hear you. I'll speak to you in a few days,' Hugh shouted, then rang off.

Ed sighed. He'd do some investigating of his own. Maybe he was wrong about the Monet.

Chapter 22

Matron Bright was nowhere to be found and the office was locked. Ed thought he might use one of the computers to do some research but none of the keys on the ring she'd given him worked. The woman wasn't lying when she said she was security conscious. Ed calculated the time difference in New York City and called his assistant, Callum Preston, to see what the young man could find out for him.

He let the studio phone ring until the answering machine picked up. It was strange to leave a message after hearing his own voice on the other end of the line.

'Callum, could you give me a ring as soon as you get this? I need you to do something for me urgently. Thanks. Oh, it's Ed.' He terminated the call.

His stomach grumbled and he realised that it was after seven thirty. He wondered if his dinner had been delivered to his room already.

Ed was walking across the Great Hall when a woman dressed in trousers and a smart white shirt buzzed her way in through the front doors. Tall and slim, with short brunette hair, she looked about forty and was carrying a small radio.

He wondered if she was an employee. Perhaps she'd have a key to the office.

'Excuse me.' Ed intercepted her at the bottom of the stairs.

She looked at him.

'Do you work here?' he asked.

Fenella Freeman was about to ask if she looked like the rest of the ridiculously smiley staff but stopped herself.

'I just thought you might because you had a swipe to get in,' Ed tried again.

'Oh, that.' Fenella realised what he was talking about. 'No, my father is one of the residents and all of the next of kin have one, in case they'd like to visit out of hours.'

'I see. Thanks, anyway,' Ed said. He held out his hand, offering for her to walk upstairs first.

'But if you're not on staff and you don't live here, may I ask what you're doing?' Fenella's detective instincts had kicked in. She'd never seen him before and he did seem a bit lost.

'I'm Ed Clifton,' he replied.

Fenella frowned and shook her head. 'Sorry, I'm afraid that means nothing to me.'

'Um, I'm a Kennington-Jones. My brother and his wife own Pelham Park,' Ed explained.

'Oh.' Fenella wondered why she'd never heard of the man before. 'I didn't realise there was a brother.'

'Probably because I was dead.'

Fenella flinched.

Ed looked sheepish. 'It's a long story.'

'Sounds intriguing,' Fenella said. 'I mean the being dead and now undead part. Were you missing?'

'I guess you could say that. I left home a long time ago and my mother died the very next night and my father thought it best if he buried us both,' Ed said. 'That's really sounding creepy, isn't it?'

'Especially if they had a funeral.' The woman opened her eyes wide in mock horror.

'Apparently so.' Ed grinned tightly.

Fenella's horrified expression was genuine this time. 'Your father must have been a monster.'

'He was a particular type of man. A lot like his own father, from the little I can remember of my grandfather,' Ed said.

Fenella wasn't surprised to hear that. It was Ed's grandfather who had kicked her father and grand-parents off the estate years before.

'So may I ask what brought you back here, after how long?' Fenella said. 'It doesn't sound like this place holds a lot of happy memories.'

'Almost forty years. I'm here because of my mother's art collection. It needs to be catalogued and disposed of,' he explained.

Fenella said nothing, wondering where this vast collection was stored.

'Heavens, I do apologise. I've been rambling and I don't even know your name,' said Ed, smiling at the woman.

'Fenella. DS Fenella Freeman.' She couldn't help herself. It was force of habit to use her rank and title. She held out her hand, which Ed took in his. He was taken aback by the strength of her grip.

A shiver ran down Ed's spine. After what he'd just found in the cellar, having a detective in the house had thrown him. 'A member of our fine constabulary. You said that you were visiting your father. What's his name?'

'Donald Freeman,' Fenella replied.

He wondered why that name rang a bell then realised that her father was the elderly gentleman Alice-Miranda had been talking to that morning. But there was something else ticking away in the back of his mind. He was sure that name meant more to him.

'Are you heading up?' Ed asked.

Fenella nodded and the two of them walked upstairs side by side.

'It was nice to meet you, DS Freeman,' Ed remarked as Fenella turned to walk down the passageway on their left. 'Freeman . . . You're not related to Niall Freeman, are you?'

Fenella stopped and turned around. 'He's my brother,' she replied tersely.

‘Oh, that’s great. Niall’s a genius. I love his work.’

‘Of course you do.’ Fenella smiled bitterly. It was always about Niall, she thought to herself.

On his way down the hall, Ed pulled out his phone and stared at the screen. With DS Freeman in the house he really wanted to speak to Callum as soon as possible.

As he pushed open the door to his room he could see a covered plate on the small table. Ed pulled off the silver cloche and was surprised to find the food still hot. He picked up the fork, stabbing at a piece of meat, before he rang home again.

He was almost ready to give up again when Callum answered.

‘Cal, is that you?’ Music blared in the background.

‘Sorry, I can’t hear you,’ Callum shouted.

‘Well, turn the volume down!’ Ed yelled.

‘Hang on a tick, I’ll just turn the volume down,’ the young man shouted. ‘Sorry about that. Callum Preston speaking.’

'Cal, it's Ed.'

'Oh, hi. Are things going well? Have you seen Alice-Miranda? Please give her my best.'

Callum was clearly up for a chat. Ed wasn't. 'Cal, I need some help and you must be very discreet about any enquiries you make.'

'Sounds serious. Anything wrong?'

'I'm not sure but I need you to investigate a painting for me. Look up *Waterloo Bridge, London*, by Monet and tell me where it hangs.'

'What are you talking about? It doesn't. It was stolen from the Kunsthal in Rotterdam,' Callum said.

'Are you sure?' Ed asked.

'Absolutely. It was all over the papers. That painting was destroyed in a fire by the thief's mother,' said Callum. 'Don't you remember? Big heist and then all that beautiful work gone.'

'Oh gosh.' Ed put the fork down on the edge of his plate. 'That's why I knew about it.'

'What are you talking about, Ed?' Callum asked.

'The good news is that the painting is in one piece,' Ed said.

'Really? How do you know?' Callum demanded.

'Because it's sitting in the cellar with my mother's collection,' Ed replied.

'Wow!' Callum gasped. 'Are you serious? What are you going to do about it?'

'I'm not sure. But you mustn't breathe a word. I can't quite believe it myself and I'm almost afraid to look at what else might be there.'

'Does Hugh know?' Callum asked.

'Not yet. He's off the grid for a few days,' said Ed. 'Not a word to anyone, Cal. Not a word, you hear me.' And with that he ended the call.

Ed's mind was in a whirl. How had a recently stolen painting worth tens of millions of dollars ended up in the cellar at Pelham Park among his mother's artworks? It just didn't make any sense at all.

Donald Freeman was dozing in front of the television when Fenella let herself into his apartment. She'd knocked but when there was no answer she used her key. Fenella walked past her father and into the kitchenette. She put the radio on the table then turned and filled a glass of water at the tap. Through the window she could see the cross on top of the rise, where the Kennington-Jones family crypt overlooked the estate. Gosh people could be cruel, she thought. Fancy Ed Clifton's father having a funeral for him when he knew full well that his son was alive. But then, perhaps cruelty ran in the family.

Fenella's mind wandered to her own grandfather and what could have happened all those years ago for him to be so heartlessly dismissed from Pelham Park. It sounded as if the Kennington-Jones elders had a lot to answer for. She'd love to know the truth.

Fenella walked back into the sitting room where her father had begun to snore – throaty grunts punctuated by whistling breaths. She removed the little black leather-bound book that was open on his chest and sat it on the table beside him. There was no point waking him. She'd call in the morning and let him know about the radio.

Chapter 23

The Barn Owls arrived back at camp just as Mr Lipp was rushing about rounding up the Winchester-Fayle Singers for choir practice.

The rest of the children were to use their spare time before dinner to have showers and tidy their rooms for an inspection that Miss Reedy had promised for that evening.

'Hurry along, everyone. Mr Trout's waiting for us in the hall,' Mr Lipp directed.

Clearly Mr Trout was rehearsing already

as pounding piano music echoed through the camp.

The children arrived in dribs and drabs. When Figgy wandered in last, fifteen minutes after the rehearsal had started, Mr Lipp looked as if he was set to explode.

'Glad you could join us, Figworth.'

The teacher was flapping his arms and strutting about like a peacock. His suit was just as colourful too, as he'd traded his beige safari gear for one of his more traditional ensembles. This time it was a pair of pink plaid trousers, a bright yellow shirt and a polka-dot cravat.

Figgy slunk into the back row and began opening and closing his mouth like a giant carp.

The song reached its explosive crescendo and Mr Lipp made the children hold the last note for far too long. Most of them lost their breath well before he cut them off. Except for Caprice, who warbled like a songbird.

'Stunning, Caprice. Absolutely beautiful. But as for the rest of you, learn to hold a note,' Mr Lipp huffed.

An hour after the rehearsal had started, Alice-Miranda put up her hand. 'Excuse me, Mr Lipp, but aren't we supposed to be at dinner?'

He looked at the clock on the wall and then at his watch. 'Oh goodness,' he blustered. 'Yes, yes. We don't want Miss Reedy sending a search party.'

The children looked sideways at one another, glad that Alice-Miranda had spoken up. The rumbling of stomachs threatened to drown out the singing.

'Off you go,' Mr Lipp said. 'We'll reconvene tomorrow.'

In the dining room, the children were greeted by Miss Reedy, who seemed remarkably relaxed. She'd been too busy with Mr Plumpton, plotting a little getaway for the end of term, to notice their lateness.

'Sorry, Miss Reedy. Mr Lipp didn't realise the time,' Alice-Miranda apologised on behalf of the group.

'Oh, goodness,' she said, glancing at her watch then at the bain-maries, which she hoped the staff hadn't already started to clear. But the children were in luck. The mystery meat and rice dish hadn't been a huge hit with the students and there was plenty left. 'Run along, everyone, you must be starving,' she said with a smile.

'What are we doing after dinner?' Alice-Miranda asked.

'I think the camp leaders have a trivia night planned,' Miss Reedy said.

Alice-Miranda grinned. 'I love trivia.'

Sloane rolled her eyes. 'Only because you're so good at it.'

'We'll see about that,' Caprice said with a smirk.

Caprice's plans to make Alice-Miranda look stupid backfired horribly. In the early rounds she fed Millie a stream of incorrect answers, which the girl reluctantly attempted to get Alice-Miranda to use. In the end Caprice was forced to change her plans. What a pity Alice-Miranda's buzzer was about to fail.

'This has been one of the most exciting trivia competitions we've ever seen at Bagley Hall,' Beth said. She and Lionel, another one of the instructors, were acting as quizmasters. They were dressed in gaudy checked jackets with pork pie hats and oversized glasses. Miss Reedy commented that she thought they looked like used car salesmen. Mr Plumpton wondered if they'd borrowed their jackets from Mr Lipp.

'Okay, so we're down to the final round and it looks like we have two Barn Owls in the lead: Caprice and Alice-Miranda,' said Beth. She led a huge round of applause.

'Go Alice-Miranda!' Sloane cheered.

'Go Caprice,' Figgy yelled.

'Girls, we need you to come out the front,' said Lionel.

Alice-Miranda and Caprice walked to the table that had been moved into place for the final. Two buzzers sat side by side. The girls took their seats and smiled at the audience.

Millie didn't say a word. She moved off to the side and looked at where the power cords for the buzzers were plugged into the socket. Her eyes followed the cords to be sure which was which.

'Now, if the first person to buzz gets the question wrong, then the other will have an opportunity to answer. Best of three,' Lionel said.

Beth moved back to the whiteboard to record the scores.

'First question. What is the capital city of Portugal?'

The girls pressed their buzzers. Alice-Miranda's flashed first.

'Yes, Alice-Miranda.' Lionel looked intently at the child.

'Lisbon,' she replied.

'Correct!'

A huge cheer went up around the room.

Caprice's eyes searched the room for Millie.

Millie had spotted her target. Fortunately, the teachers were too busy drinking tea and watching the competition to notice her.

'Second question. This is a history one. Name the Egyptian pharaoh responsible for the building of the Great Pyramid of Giza.'

Both girls jammed their hands on the buzzers, but Caprice made it first.

'Yes, Caprice?'

The girl smiled sweetly. 'Khufu.'

'Well done!'

The children cheered wildly again.

'Okay, this is it. The third and final question. Whoever gets this right wins the title of Bagley Hall Quiz Champion – well, for this week anyway.' Lionel grinned.

Miss Reedy stood up from her seat at the teachers' table and addressed the students. 'Settle down, everyone. Before we finish I'd just like to say that both girls have been very impressive and we will be taking their performances into account when adding up today's individual scores.'

'But the winner gets more points, don't they?' Caprice demanded.

'Yes, of course,' said Miss Reedy slowly. She was a little surprised by the girl's tone.

Caprice smiled at the teacher then glared at Millie, who was still crouched next to the power points.

'Last question.' Lionel couldn't believe that he was using the cards generally reserved for students in high school. These little girls were amazing. 'What is the longest river in the world?'

The girls hit their buzzers simultaneously but only Caprice's lit up.

'Caprice.' Lionel looked at the girl through his oversized quizmaster glasses.

'The Amazon,' Caprice replied smugly.

Lionel bit his lip and looked at his card. 'I'm afraid that's incorrect.'

Caprice's jaw hit the ground. 'It can't be wrong. I know these things.'

Lionel looked at Alice-Miranda. 'Do you know?'

The child nodded. 'I think so. Is it the Nile?' She looked at Lionel expectantly.

'It's the Nile!' Lionel shouted and the crowd went crazy. The young man walked over and raised Alice-Miranda's hand in the air.

Caprice's face was as dark as a moonless night.

Alice-Miranda looked about for Millie and gave her friend a wave. Millie gave a half-hearted smile. She wondered what evil plan Caprice was plotting for her punishment. It wasn't her fault the stupid girl didn't know the answer. She'd done what she was asked, and it sickened her to the core.

Alice-Miranda turned to Caprice and held out her hand. 'Thanks for a great match.'

Caprice turned her head the other way. But when she spotted Beth frowning at her, she quickly turned back to Alice-Miranda and grabbed her hand. She shook it vigorously then leaned across and gave the tiny child a hug too.

'You were fantastic,' Caprice simpered.

'Thanks, Caprice. You were pretty amazing yourself.'

Beth presented Alice-Miranda with a tiny plastic trophy.

Miss Reedy stood and walked to the front. Judging by the contagious yawns that were spreading around the room, Miss Reedy was hopeful that the children would have an early night and her hallway patrols would be over quickly. She was feeling quite tired herself. She tapped the microphone and addressed the students.

'Well done, everyone. What a marvellous evening we've had. Now, just before we go Miss Wall is going to update the team scores. Any treats will be held over until tomorrow. No midnight feasts, I'm afraid.'

A groan spread around the room.

'And the leader of the teams competition tonight is . . . drumroll please . . .'

The children pounded their feet on the carpet.

'The Robins!'

High-pitched squeals almost perforated eardrums as the youngest students celebrated their success.

'See, I told you everyone will get a win at some stage,' Jacinta told Sloane. 'Hope it's us soon. I could do with some chocolate.'

Chapter 24

'Hello Matron Bright,' Alice-Miranda greeted the woman as she led the line of Barn Owls into the Great Hall at Pelham Park.

'Good morning, children,' the matron warbled. 'What a treat to have so many helpers – this week especially.'

The children were quickly directed to their activities. They were continuing on from yesterday for the first hour then they were to help make signs for the fair.

Alice-Miranda skipped into the reading room. 'Hello Mr Freeman.'

He yawned and stretched his back then sat up straight in his chair. 'Excuse me. How's your camp going?'

The child's smile broadened. 'We went rock climbing and learned archery and then we had a trivia contest, which was lots of fun,' she babbled. 'What did you do last night?'

'Same thing I do every night,' Donald replied, but he didn't elaborate.

Alice-Miranda fished around in her bag for her pen and paper. 'Do you mind if I ask you some more questions?' She put the paper on the table in front of her. 'You don't have to answer if you don't want to, but I think it would be lovely if your stories were mentioned at the fair.'

Donald nodded.

'What's your happiest memory of living at Pelham Park when you were young?' Alice-Miranda asked.

Donald paused for a few moments. 'The woods and the lake,' he said finally.

'Can you tell me more about your friend Harry?' Alice-Miranda asked.

At the mention of the boy's name, Donald's seawater eyes glazed over. 'We were inseparable, Harry and me. He showed me things.'

'What sort of things?' Alice-Miranda asked.

'Secret places.'

'Really – what sort of secret places?' the child asked eagerly.

'We could get in and out of this house anytime we wanted, Harry and me. And no one knew how except us.' A smile crept onto his lips.

'Are there tunnels?' she asked, wide-eyed. She was remembering how excited she was to find out that there was a labyrinth of tunnels beneath her own family home, Highton Hall.

Donald shook his head. 'No, of course not.'

'What else did you and Harry get up to?'

Donald looked at Alice-Miranda as if she was made of glass. She noticed that his breathing was shallow and deep frown lines crisscrossed his forehead. The man's eyes filled with tears. 'I didn't do it. I promise I didn't.'

'Are you all right, Mr Freeman?' Alice-Miranda wondered if he was reliving an awful memory.

Donald began to shake. 'I swear, Father, it wasn't me. It was Harry – he made me take the blame.'

Alice-Miranda looked around for Matron Bright.

'Mr Freeman, can I get you a glass of water?' she whispered.

'What?'

'A glass of water?' Alice-Miranda pushed her chair back and stood up.

Donald pulled a handkerchief from his trouser pocket and wiped his eyes.

And then, as if nothing had happened, he sat up straight. 'I don't want to talk any more.' He pulled the newspaper on the table towards him.

Alice-Miranda watched as Mr Freeman lost himself in the pages. It was as if she had disappeared.

She decided to go and find Matron Bright. Mr Freeman was obviously not well.

As she crossed the Great Hall she spotted her uncle talking with the matron near the main stairs and scurried over to meet them.

'Hello Uncle Ed, Matron Bright,' she said.

'Hello gorgeous girl,' said Ed. He leaned down and Alice-Miranda gave him a hug.

'Is anything the matter, dear?' Matron Bright asked.

'Mr Freeman was telling me some stories about when he was a boy on the estate and I'm afraid he became quite upset.' Alice-Miranda relayed the rest of what had happened.

'Oh dear. I've been worried about him lately. He seems to be losing himself in the past more and more often. The other evening he was talking to me just fine then all of a sudden he began saying something about Harry and a gun. But then he clammed up. I wonder who this Harry was. He seems to have had a big influence on Donald's early life, and I suspect it wasn't all positive.' Matron Bright shook her head. 'But don't worry, dear, I'll take him a cup of tea. Why don't you go and help your uncle for a little while.'

Alice-Miranda looked at Ed expectantly. 'May I?' she asked.

'I don't see why not,' the man replied. Ed wasn't overly concerned about the Monet. Alice-Miranda would have no idea that it didn't belong to them. Besides, he was planning on a quick trip to the attic first to see if there were any records of the paintings up there. Two pairs of eyes would be better than one.

'I'll let Mr Plumpton know where you are. Just make sure you're back up here in time for craft at eleven,' Matron Bright said with another of her smiles.

'Thank you,' Alice-Miranda said, and the woman bustled away.

Chapter 25

Alice-Miranda had never been in the attics at Pelham Park. She and Uncle Ed climbed the main stairs and walked past a row of apartments. At the end of the hall was a door, which Ed unlocked to reveal a staircase. They climbed to the top where a landing led to a central hallway with rooms off either side.

'This is where the unmarried servants used to live when I was a boy,' Ed explained.

The pair poked their heads into the first few rooms, which were filled with filing cabinets and boxes.

'How am I ever going to find what I need?' Ed groaned. 'I could search this place for a month.'

'We could split up,' Alice-Miranda suggested. 'Tell me what you're after.'

'Any records of the art collection, bills of sale, correspondence with galleries, that sort of thing,' Ed directed.

'Okay,' Alice-Miranda said. 'You start on that side and I'll start on this side.'

He grinned. 'Very well, young lady. You're a terribly good organiser, you know. Maybe you could come and get my studio sorted.'

Alice-Miranda smiled and disappeared into the first room, where she opened a dusty metal filing cabinet. Whoever had kept the family records was very neat. The files were labelled and in alphabetical order. The first drawer was dedicated to the gardens, with records of equipment purchases, the cost of garden works and even which months things were to be planted.

After going through another two drawers, there was no sign of anything to do with the artworks. Alice-Miranda moved to the next cabinet. She pulled out the first drawer. 'Staff' was the title on the first file.

She flicked through the alphabetical list until she reached F, then searched for Freeman.

Alice-Miranda's heart skipped a beat as she pulled out the file and sat it on a little table in the corner of the room. She scanned the first note's curly swirly writing, searching for clues as to why the family had left the estate.

'Oh,' she gasped. 'That's awful.'

Ed Clifton poked his head into the room. 'What's awful, darling?'

'I think you should read this,' she said.

But before he could, her uncle spotted something else. Stacked in the corner of the room was a pile of archive boxes. Marked on the front of the one at the top was the word 'Artworks'.

'Hang on a tick, Alice-Miranda.' He grabbed a stool and climbed up, then brought the box down to the table below.

'Is that what you were looking for?' she asked.

'We'll soon see.' Ed lifted the lid and pulled out the first paper. It was an invoice from a gallery.

'Bingo!' He grinned. 'Come on. We'd better get downstairs or it will be time for you to go back to Matron Bright.'

Ed replaced the lid and was out the door before

Alice-Miranda could say another word. She folded the paper she held into her pocket then scurried after him.

They reached the bottom of the main stairs just as Fenella Freeman entered the house. She was surprised to see Ed Clifton and a little girl, who looked vaguely familiar, coming towards her.

'Good morning, DS Freeman,' Ed said forcing a smile to his lips. Clearly she was a frequent visitor.

'Hello again,' she said.

'Hello Detective Freeman,' Alice-Miranda greeted the woman cheerily. 'You probably don't remember but I'm Alice-Miranda Highton-Smith-Kennington-Jones and I was on the bus the other afternoon. This is my Uncle Ed but it looks as if you've already met.'

Fenella studied the child. So that's where she'd seen her. She would have preferred not to remember the unstolen bus incident. 'Mmm, of course.'

'Your father's in the reading room. I think he might be a little bit tired,' the child explained.

Fenella had forgotten to bring the cord for the radio when she dropped it off the night before. Things at the station were deathly quiet so she'd taken the opportunity to slip out for a while. Besides, the two young constables she worked with, Wilson and Barker, were driving her insane with their constant quips and bickering.

She couldn't believe she'd felt so sorry for Ed Clifton when she met him yesterday. He might have been abandoned by his father but she'd done a little digging on him when she got home and his life didn't look too bad. Apparently he was one of New York's most celebrated artists. It seemed to Fenella that she was surrounded by them – just to remind her of what might have been, if only she hadn't been so afraid.

'Well, we'll see you later,' said Ed, nodding at the woman. His arms were beginning to strain under the weight of the box.

'We're going to look at Granny's art collection,' Alice-Miranda said. 'It's in the cellars.'

'Really?' Fenella couldn't help but wonder what priceless treasures were down there.

'Come on, Alice-Miranda. If we don't get moving it will be time for you to go back to camp,' her uncle urged. 'And we don't want to take up DS Freeman's time. I'm sure she has lots of important things to do. Catching criminals and all that.'

I wish, Fenella thought to herself. Dunleavy was hardly a hotbed of unlawful activity.

'Actually, I'd love to see your collection,' the policewoman said. 'If you've got time for a quick tour?'

Ed felt his heart jump.

'Oh, it's such a jumble down there. Just a bunch of dusty old paintings.' Ed grinned. 'You'll get terribly dirty.'

She glanced at her watch. 'I don't mind.' She had nothing urgent that afternoon. Just more paperwork and putting up with those morons at the station.

'Come on, Uncle Ed, you can show us both,' Alice-Miranda said.

Ed Clifton took a deep breath. Fenella Freeman was a detective in tiny old Dunleavy. It was unlikely that she had her finger on the pulse of stolen art treasures from around the world. Besides, at some point Ed would have to let the authorities know. Just not yet.

'Okay, follow me.' Ed walked to the far corner of the entrance foyer and down a long passageway. Alice-Miranda and Fenella followed.

They reached the end of the hall and Ed trotted down the back staircase and through the old kitchen to the butler's pantry, where he unlocked the door.

Fenella Freeman looked around in awe. Obviously this part of the house wasn't used any more.

She was imagining what it must have been like in years gone by when the place was crowded with servants. She assumed her grandfather would have spent a lot of time downstairs performing his duties as a butler.

'What was it like growing up here?' Fenella asked Ed. 'I can't imagine having such a vast house for just one family.'

'To tell you the truth, I didn't know any different back then. I probably thought everyone lived in grand mansions and had an army of servants and their own nanny. But of course, when I went off to school and started going home with friends for holidays I realised that this life was far from normal. I adored my mother but my father, well, I think I mentioned last night that he wasn't the easiest of people to be around.'

Ed unlocked the door at the bottom of the stairs. He'd left the lights on when he was down there earlier in the morning.

Fenella scanned the mountains of bric-a-brac. 'Have you thought about having a yard sale?'

'Yes, my sister-in-law suggested we should sell some of it off at the fair on Saturday. The locals might be interested in some souvenirs from the house,'

Ed said. 'But I think it might take until next year's anniversary to get it sorted out.'

'You can keep *him*,' Fenella said with a shudder. She was glaring at the polar bear.

'That's Sidney,' Ed said. 'He used to live in Father's study. When I was very little I was petrified of him but as I grew older he and I became friends. I often prayed he might come to life and eat Father while he was at his desk, but it never worked.'

'Uncle Ed, that's a terrible thing to say!' Alice-Miranda chastised.

Fenella Freeman laughed. 'It would have made for an interesting murder investigation!'

Ed turned to his niece and raised his eyebrows. 'You didn't know my father, Alice-Miranda.'

Ed walked to the vault door and put the archive box down on the floor. He twirled the lock and pulled the metal face forward. Alice-Miranda and Fenella walked through.

'Wow!' Alice-Miranda exclaimed. 'This is amazing.'

Fenella Freeman's eyes were on stalks. She'd never seen such a vast collection in one small space.

'Why did Grandpa put it all down here?' Alice-Miranda asked.

'He never liked art. Thought it was a waste of money. And I suppose when Mother died it was a painful reminder. Like I said before, Alice-Miranda, your grandfather was a hard man.'

'Isn't that a Picasso?' The child pointed at a cubist painting of a bull.

'Sure is,' Ed replied.

Fenella rolled her eyes. That painting alone was probably worth millions. She was impressed that the child knew what it was, but then again, it was just as likely there were Picassos hanging on her bedroom wall.

'What can I do to help, Uncle Ed?' Alice-Miranda asked. She noticed a clipboard with paper and a pen, and a long list of names and artists.

Ed was anxious to get Detective Freeman back upstairs as quickly as possible. He glanced at his watch. 'Actually, sweetheart, what time did your teacher want you?'

'Eleven,' the child said.

'It's quarter to and it will take us a good ten minutes to make our way upstairs. We should probably go.'

'Maybe Matron Bright will let me come back again,' Alice-Miranda suggested. She spotted a shiny gold wrapper on the floor and bent down to pick it up. It smelt like chocolate. She stuffed it in her pocket.

Ed was watching Detective Freeman closely as she wandered through the racks, pulling some of the artwork forward to get a better look.

Fenella couldn't believe what she was seeing. Her father had often taken her and her brother to galleries when they were young. She remembered how he used to declare, 'One day I'm going to own that piece.' They'd laugh at him. Especially when they realised it was a Rembrandt or a Constable or something worth more than their house and possibly every other house in their street too.

Fenella remembered asking her father why he didn't just buy prints of the things he liked but he said that was cheating. He would only ever have the real thing and if he couldn't have that then he would prefer to have nothing at all.

And here were the real deals. Dozens of them, by the looks of things.

'Well, come on then,' said Ed. He turned to leave.

Just as Fenella was about to follow him, something caught her eye. A landscape. It looked familiar.

After a moment she realised it was a Turner. He was one of her father's favourites.

Ed saw it too. He was sure his mother had owned a Turner . . . or had she? He couldn't be certain and he'd only been through a small number of the works so far. His stomach knotted.

'Come on. You don't want to be late, Alice-Miranda.' Ed stepped aside and allowed Fenella to exit first. But his niece remained in the far corner of the room, staring at a different canvas.

'Uncle Ed, can you come here for a minute?' she called.

He walked around the first two rows of racks and found the child in front of a colourful painting.

'What is it?' he asked.

She pointed at the painting and pulled on her uncle's sleeve. The man leaned down.

She cupped her hands and whispered in his ear. 'That painting's very famous.'

Ed gulped and nodded his head. A vein in his forehead began to throb.

'Do you know why?' she asked.

The man nodded again.

'What's it doing here?' she asked.

Ed shrugged. 'Come along, darling. We really must get you upstairs,' he said loudly.

Alice-Miranda gave her uncle a knowing look and they made a dash for the doorway.

Ed picked up the archive box and was relieved to find Fenella Freeman waiting at the bottom of the stairs. He hoped she hadn't been anywhere close just now, even though Alice-Miranda had kept her voice down.

Ed locked each door behind them and the three made their way to the reading room.

Chapter 26

'There you are, Alice-Miranda,' said Mr Plumpton. He walked towards the trio. 'We need to get going. Miss Reedy telephoned to say that she's had to reshuffle some of the group activities and we're now scheduled to go canoeing this afternoon and have our sleep-out.'

Alice-Miranda desperately wanted to speak with her uncle in private.

'I think your father's in the reading room, Detective Freeman,' Alice-Miranda said, hoping that the woman would be eager to see him.

Fenella nodded her thanks, but before she could move off, Matron Bright bustled along the hall, carrying a stack of cardboard. 'Oh hello there, everyone,' she warbled. 'If you're looking for your father, DS Freeman, he's gone up to his apartment. He said he wasn't feeling well and I'm afraid he's had another one of his little episodes.'

Fenella frowned. She turned to Ed and Alice-Miranda. 'Thanks for the tour.' She headed for her father's apartment, unable to shake the feeling that she'd seen that Turner painting somewhere before. Perhaps her father had pointed it out during one of their gallery visits.

'Are the children in the craft room, Mr Plumpton?' Matron Bright asked, eager to get started on the signs for the fair.

The teacher should his head. 'No, I was just coming to find you. We have to head back now due to a change in the program but I believe Miss Wall's group will be over shortly.'

'Lovely,' she said. 'And how are you getting on, Mr Clifton? Is there anything you need?'

'No, matron. I'm fine, thank you,' Ed replied. But that was far from the truth.

Matron Bright smiled and scooted away to the craft room.

'Say goodbye to your uncle, Alice-Miranda,' said Mr Plumpton. 'We'll be back again tomorrow.' And with that the teacher strode across the foyer and outside to meet the waiting group of students.

'Uncle Ed, what are you going to do?' Alice-Miranda asked urgently. 'Shouldn't we tell Detective Freeman?'

'Not yet, I need to see what else I can find,' Ed replied. 'But how did you recognise that painting?'

Ed Clifton knew that his only niece was an incredibly perceptive child but he found it hard to believe that she could identify stolen artwork.

'We did a project on Rubens last year and our teacher found some old newspaper articles about a robbery. I thought it was fascinating that something like that could just disappear out of a museum in broad daylight, so I did some more research. It's been gone for quite a few years,' the child explained.

Ed nodded. 'It's not the only one.'

Alice-Miranda's brown eyes were the size of saucers. 'What do you mean?'

'I found another. Last night.'

'Another Rubens?' Alice-Miranda asked.

'No, it's a Monet,' the man replied.

'Have you told Daddy?'

'I tried but he's away until tonight,' Ed replied. 'I have to be sure that those are the only two paintings that don't belong to Mother's collection,' Ed said. 'I suspect there could be at least one more.' He couldn't stop thinking about the Turner landscape that DS Freeman had just spotted.

'Alice-Miranda!' Millie peered in from the main door. 'Mr Plumpton's frothing at the mouth out here. You need to hurry up!'

'Coming!' Alice-Miranda called back.

'You'd better go, sweetheart. I'll see you tomorrow and hopefully by then I might have figured some of this out,' Ed said with a deep sigh.

Alice-Miranda gave him a hug. 'Don't worry, Uncle Ed. There's got to be a sensible explanation.'

But Ed Clifton wasn't so sure. Possession of stolen goods was a criminal offence and at the moment the paintings in that basement were in the possession of his brother and sister-in-law.

Chapter 27

Several of the Barn Owls scurried along beside Mr Plumpton as the short man trotted to Bagley Hall. He was fully aware that they were running much later than they should have been.

'Where are we camping, Mr Plumpton? Figgy asked.

'Somewhere along the river,' the teacher answered.

Sloane scoffed. 'That's stupid. Why do we have to sleep in a tent when we have perfectly good beds inside Bagley Hall?'

The teacher looked at the girl. Personally he quite agreed and wasn't looking forward to an evening on the ground, but he could hardly say so. 'It's about the experience, Sloane. You will have to pitch your tent, make a campfire and cook your own meals, as well as digging a toilet. Passing this test is a big part of your Queen's Blue.'

'Oh, gross,' Sloane sighed. 'I just won't go.'

'But you have to. As I said, it's part of the challenge,' Mr Plumpton chided.

'Not the camp, Mr Plumpton,' Sloane said, shaking her head. 'The toilet. I won't be going to the toilet while we're out there.'

'Oh, I see.' Mr Plumpton frowned. He'd been wondering about that himself and hardly relishing the thought.

'Good luck with that,' Rufus said. 'Especially if we're cooking our own dinner. I've always found that stew equals p–'

Mr Plumpton cut the lad off. 'Pemberley, must you always be so . . . so base?' The teacher sighed and shook his head. Having travelled to Paris with some of the boys from Fayle and now this camp, the man was very glad that he worked in a girls' school. Dealing constantly with toilet humour and unpleasant smells was not his idea of fun.

Sloane shuddered. 'You're gross, Figgy.'

Millie glanced around, wondering where Alice-Miranda had got to. She spied her at the back of the group on her own. Millie stopped and waited for her friend to catch up.

'Are you all right?' Millie asked.

Alice-Miranda nodded.

'You looked like you were somewhere else. When you get like that I wonder if there's something you're not telling me,' Millie said.

'I was thinking about Mr Freeman. This morning he was talking about a boy called Harry who was his best friend on the estate but it sounded like something terrible had happened between them. And then I found this when I was in the attic with Uncle Ed.' Alice-Miranda pulled the piece of paper out of her pocket.

'What is it?' Millie asked. The handwriting was very old-fashioned and she could hardly make out any of the words.

'It's a note about Mr Freeman's father, saying that he was dismissed from the estate because of an incident where a horse was killed.'

'That's horrible,' said Millie.

'Mr Freeman got very upset this morning. He said something about it not being his fault – that

Harry made him take the blame. I wonder if it was something to do with this, but the second page is missing. Can you imagine your best friend blaming you for something they did?'

The red-haired girl gulped. Alice-Miranda was her best friend in the world – someone Millie imagined she would be friends with forever. She couldn't believe she'd agreed to help Caprice with her plan to win the medal. 'No, it's too horrible for words.'

Caprice had fallen back to listen in on their conversation. Sappy little creatures. How sad for that old man to have a friend and then not have him any more. Wouldn't that be terrible? She smiled to herself. Millie was about to find out just how terrible that was.

Millie handed the page back to Alice-Miranda.

But Alice-Miranda hadn't told Millie everything. She was worried about Mr Freeman and what she'd found in the attic, but she was even more perplexed about the painting in the cellar. If only she could spend the night at the house and help her uncle sort things out.

Fenella Freeman knocked on the door of her father's apartment.

'Coming,' he called, and opened the door a few seconds later.

'Hi Dad.' Fenella held up the cable in her hand. 'I forgot the lead for the radio.'

'What radio?' the old man asked as she walked inside.

The woman sighed. 'The one I left for you last night, Dad. It's in the kitchen.'

'Oh, of course.' Donald hurried after her. He picked up a small leather-bound book from the table beside his reclining chair and slammed it shut, hoping his daughter hadn't noticed it.

Fortunately Fenella walked straight through to the kitchen.

'Dad,' she called. 'Do you remember a Turner painting that you once took Niall and me to see?'

Donald stuffed the book between the couch cushions and walked into the kitchen.

'There are a lot of Turners, Fen. He was prolific. And we've probably seen hundreds of them.' Donald wondered where this conversation was coming from and where it was going.

'I thought it had an opposite too – it was part of a pair, I think,' said Fenella. The cloudy memory swirling at the back of her mind was starting to focus.

'Sorry, Fen, I don't remember.' Donald shook his head and went to put the kettle on.

'*Light and Colour*! That's it!' Fenella clapped her hands together.

Donald felt a shiver run down his spine. 'Really?' he said. 'Why do you ask?'

'I just went downstairs with Ed Clifton. Have you met him? He's Hugh Kennington-Jones's long-lost brother. I'm sure you must have heard of him. He's a painter – does some really attractive work, by the looks of what I saw online. He offered to give me a tour of his mother's art collection in the cellar and, I don't know why, but I thought it would be interesting. I've just been down there and as soon as I saw this one, something sparked. It's there, Dad. *Light and Colour* by Turner. They own it,' Fenella frothed.

'It's probably just a reproduction,' her father said. He was standing in front of the sink and staring out the window.

'I don't think so. There's so much art down there. I mean, there's one giant jumbled room full of furniture and then there's this room with a steel door and a combination lock, with racks and racks of artwork. Seriously, how does one family have so much?' Fenella griped. 'Anyway, I thought you'd like to know, seeing as you always loved that one. Perhaps Ed will take you down to have a look if you ask him.'

Donald gulped. 'I don't think so, Fen. My old legs are playing up a lot at the moment. I can barely get up and down the stairs.'

'Come on, Dad. You're all right. I know there wasn't much time for galleries when Mum was sick but you could have gone back to it, you know. Don't tell me you don't miss it.' Fenella walked over and stood shoulder to shoulder with her father.

'Would you like a cuppa?' the old man asked, ignoring his daughter's question.

Fenella glanced at the clock and realised that she'd been gone far longer than she'd intended. 'Sorry, Dad, I'd better get back. Besides, I want to do some research and see when the Kennington-Joneses bought that painting. I'm sure I saw it somewhere with you when I was a child. But Ed mentioned that his mother died forty years ago. That can't be right. You have to wonder about these people.

Priceless artworks and they don't even hang them on the walls. More money than sense, wouldn't you say?'

Fenella turned and gave her father a peck on the cheek.

'I'll see you in a couple of days. The radio's set up, Dad. You just need to turn the dial and tune into whichever station you're keen on these days.'

'What was he doing down there?' Donald asked as Fenella turned to leave.

'They're selling the collection,' Fenella replied. 'He mentioned something about cataloguing and getting it ready for disposal. I told you. You should ask him to take you for a look before it's all gone.'

Donald nodded and closed his eyes. He'd known it would happen one day. He'd just hoped it would be long after he'd gone. He heard the door close and waited a minute before he walked back into the sitting room. He dug his hand in between the cushions and pulled out the small black book. Donald shook his head. His daughter had wanted a big case. And here it was – about to land in her lap. But he couldn't let it happen.

Chapter 28

The Barn Owls had fifteen minutes to pack a change of clothes and their sleeping bags into their day packs. Fortunately they wouldn't have to carry their food as well, as the camp staff would drop that off at the camp site.

The sun had dipped behind some fat grey clouds and Mr Plumpton sensed a change in the wind. He hoped they weren't in for a wet night. That was all they needed.

'Hello Mr Plumpton,' said Miss Reedy as

she spotted the teacher in the quadrangle.

'Oh, hello Miss Reedy.' Mr Plumpton couldn't help but smile broadly.

'Sorry about the change of plans with the canoeing,' she said, sighing. 'Mr Lipp insisted that he couldn't have the children out tomorrow night as he needed another rehearsal with the choir before the fair. Honestly, you'd think they were performing for the Queen. As far as I can tell, there'll be a lot of people from the village and the residents of Pelham Park and that's about it. If Harry had his way, those children would be practising all jolly day and half the night.'

'Don't worry yourself, Livinia,' Mr Plumpton said. 'I just hope he hasn't been bothering you too much.'

'You have nothing to worry about, Josiah,' Miss Reedy confirmed. 'Mr Lipp could be Lawrence Ridley's twin brother and it wouldn't change a thing about the way I feel.'

Hearing those words made Josiah's heart soar.

'What was that you were saying about me being Lawrence Ridley's twin brother?' Harold Lipp said cheerily as he approached the pair. He smoothed his safari suit and winked at Miss Reedy. 'I had no idea you'd seen the resemblance.'

Mr Plumpton bit his tongue.

Miss Reedy smothered a grin and said, 'Pity you don't have the same fashion sense.'

'Yes, I quite agree. The poor man looks as if he could do with some styling. I'd be happy to offer a few tips next time he pops in to see Lucas at school,' Mr Lipp boasted.

Several of the children had arrived in the quadrangle. Mr Lipp was waiting to speak with Caprice about a song.

'Have a lovely time, Mr Plumpton,' Miss Reedy said quietly, and reached out to give his arm a gentle squeeze. 'I wish I was able to join you,' she whispered.

Mr Plumpton's nose glowed red. 'Have a good evening, Miss Reedy.' He beamed as she skipped off to check on Miss Wall's Hawks at the swimming pool.

Figgy appeared at that moment. 'When are you going to ask her to marry you, sir?'

Harold Lipp did a double take. 'Figworth, that's none of your business.'

'Not you, Mr Lipp. Miss Reedy doesn't fancy you at all. I was talking to Mr Plumpton.' The boy rolled his eyes.

'I knew that,' Mr Lipp huffed. 'And don't be ridiculous anyway.'

Josiah Plumpton stared the man down. 'Why would that be ridiculous, Mr Lipp?'

'Well, there are more reasons than I care to count. For a start, Miss Reedy's a woman of the world. She's well read and extremely bright and she's deserving of someone who can, well, complement her,' Mr Lipp blathered.

'And I don't?' Mr Plumpton demanded.

'No offence, Josiah, but you're hardly a catch, are you?' Mr Lipp sniffed. He hadn't realised that the rest of the Barn Owls had now arrived and were eagerly listening to the teachers' conversation.

'That's not true. Mr Plumpton's a great catch,' said Alice-Miranda.

Jacinta leapt to the teacher's defence too. 'He's smart and he's sweet and he loves his work – even if he does blow things up quite a bit. I'd say that makes his lessons even more interesting.'

Josiah Plumpton beamed.

Mr Lipp was flummoxed. 'You have no idea what we were talking about, Jacinta, and I'll thank you to keep your opinions to yourself.' He turned and strode off across the quadrangle, completely forgetting why he'd been waiting there in the first place.

A few minutes later he sheepishly returned. 'Caprice, may I see you please?'

Mr Lipp handed her a sheet and asked if he could possibly impose on her to learn the song before the next day's rehearsal.

'Of course, Mr Lipp,' Caprice said. 'It will be a pleasure. And might I say, sir, that I think you and Miss Reedy would make a lovely couple.'

The teacher smiled at her. 'It's good to know that *some* people around here have decent taste.' And with that he hurried away.

Mr Plumpton stood beside Beth. 'Come along, everyone. Beth is going to explain the activities you're about to undertake . . .'

Fenella Freeman arrived back at the station to find the place locked and a note from Wilson and Barker saying that they'd been called out to an accident on the motorway. She wondered why both of them had to attend, particularly when she learned that it was a single-vehicle incident involving a little old lady who'd run off the road into the median strip and become bogged. Hardly a major event. She glanced at the pile of paperwork on Barker's desk. Those two were the laziest creatures to walk the earth as far as she was concerned.

She didn't care, though. It was nice to have the station to herself. Fenella sat down in front of the computer and jiggled the mouse to bring the screen back to life. She typed the words 'Light and Colour Turner' into the search engine and waited. A vast number of hits appeared. She added the name 'Kennington-Jones' and waited but nothing came up.

Fenella decided to search for the history of ownership. She scanned the first site and realised where her father had taken her and Niall to view the painting. What came next had her eyes glued to the screen and made her heart thump in her chest.

Stolen? Really? She searched the police database too, taking extra care to check whether the painting had been found and returned to its owners or whether it was still an open case. She wasn't about to go off half-cocked again.

The telephone rang. Fenella picked it up and her ears were immediately assaulted by shrieking.

'DS Freeman, how may I help?' she asked.

The woman on the other end sobbed hysterically. Fenella couldn't understand what she was saying for the first few minutes and had to ask her to calm down and take a breath. When she finally got her words out, all Fenella could hear was 'murdered'.

The detective leapt out of her chair and snatched up a notepad. 'Your address?' she demanded. Fenella scribbled the details on the pad.

The painting would have to wait. It seemed that life in Dunleavy had suddenly become a lot more interesting than it had been for a very long time.

Chapter 29

The Barn Owls traipsed through the woods with Beth in the lead and Mr Plumpton bringing up the rear. It wasn't long before the overhanging branches opened up and the children found themselves on the pebbly banks of a pretty river.

Further along, a row of upturned yellow canoes sat side by side. High on the bank behind them was a small shed with its roller door open.

'Okay, everyone. I need you to go and get a life jacket and a paddle from the shed. Your life jacket should fit nice and snug and come down to your hips. I don't want to see any that you're wearing as dresses and none that look like midriff tops either,' Beth instructed.

'How many people in each canoe?' Rufus called.

'Three, so please arrange yourselves in groups,' Beth replied.

The children looked at one another. There were ten students in the Barn Owls.

'What about the odd man out?' Caprice asked. She wasn't planning for that to be her.

'Mr Plumpton and I will be in the mix too,' said Beth. 'Perhaps, Mr Plumpton, we should appoint a leader for each group and then they can choose their crew?' Beth suggested.

'Mmm, good idea,' the teacher replied. 'Our four leaders are . . .' He looked at the children and thought about who should have a turn. 'Susannah, Lucas, Caprice and Sep. Now select your shipmates.'

The teacher pointed his finger at Susannah, who chose Sloane. Lucas then chose Jacinta and everyone groaned.

'Of course he'd choose his girlfriend,' Figgy guffawed.

Caprice pointed at Millie and Sep selected Alice-Miranda. Millie's stomach knotted. She'd been hoping her telepathic messages to Susannah and Lucas might have saved her spending another activity with Caprice.

Susannah then pointed at Beth. Lucas *ummed* and *ahhed* between Figgy and Rufus before deciding on the latter. The lad was strong and he should be a good paddler. Caprice picked Figgy, who almost keeled over on the spot. It left Mr Plumpton to go with Alice-Miranda and Sep.

The children heaved and shoved their canoes to the river's edge, loaded their belongings and started to paddle upstream. The tents were being delivered to a protected spot on the edge of the woods near the boundary between Bagley Hall and Pelham Park. The camp site was only a few hundred metres away from where they were setting out, but the children didn't know that yet.

'Okay,' Beth called from her spot at the front of Susannah's canoe. 'Try to stay together. I don't want anyone going too far ahead nor lagging behind. You'll get the hang of the paddling. Just make sure that you don't all paddle on the same side.'

'Why? What happens then?' Rufus asked, swapping his paddle to the same side as his partners just to see. Their canoe starting turning in a circle.

'Hey, what are you doing?' Lucas called over his shoulder to the boy.

Jacinta quickly swapped her paddle to the other side and the canoe surged forward again.

'Oh, you go around in circles,' Rufus said.

'Is he really as dumb as he makes out?' Caprice muttered.

A few minutes later Susannah, Sloane and Beth had got themselves caught up in some overhanging branches and Sloane was busy yelling at everyone that it wasn't her fault.

It seemed that the only group who really had their act together was Caprice's.

The children paddled upstream for an hour before Beth instructed them to turn around and head back to their camp site.

Millie rubbed her aching arms and Figgy could barely paddle another stroke. Caprice had spent the whole time rubbernecking to see what everyone else was up to, and whispering her expectations for the rest of the afternoon and evening in Millie's ear.

'When we get to camp, Millie, I expect you to help *somebody* fail every single challenge,' Caprice hissed. 'If you want her stay in one piece, that is.'

'You're disgusting,' Millie mouthed.

Figgy turned around from where he was sitting at the front of the canoe.

'What are you talking about?'

'Nothing!' Millie and Caprice snapped in unison.

'Oh, I get it.' Figgy grinned and raised his eyebrows at Caprice, who grimaced.

Millie burst out laughing. 'You know, you two would make a really cute couple.'

Caprice glared at Millie.

Figgy's heart thumped and his sigh sounded like air escaping from a balloon.

Beth pointed at the bank and told them all to head in. There was a small shelter with a table and a large flat area perfect for pitching the tents.

Several of the children realised that they had recently passed the shed they'd set out from.

'Pretty lame camp-out, sir,' Rufus complained. He pointed to the chimney pots of Pelham Park in the distance. 'Hey Alice-Miranda, are there any outside toilets over there?'

Alice-Miranda shrugged. 'I'm not sure.'

'It'd be better than digging a hole,' Rufus said, pulling a face.

The children hauled the canoes onto the bank and unpacked their things. Alice-Miranda wondered if Caprice was going to ask Millie to be her tent partner. She was pleased that the two of them seemed to be getting on better but Caprice was insistent that Millie should go with Alice-Miranda.

'There are several tests that you'll be graded on this afternoon,' Beth announced. 'The first one is putting up a tent. I'm going to demonstrate first and then you'll have ten minutes to put up the tent you'll be sleeping in with your partner.'

Caprice looked at Millie. 'You know what you have to do,' Caprice whispered to the girl as she slunk past.

Beth had a stopwatch ready. 'Okay. On your marks, get set, go!'

Alice-Miranda had the tent out of its carry bag in a few seconds. Millie unrolled it on the ground and took a few minutes to sort out which direction the door was facing. She handed Alice-Miranda two pegs and hid the others under the carry bag, but the child was a born problem solver and soon found them. This was going to be much harder than Millie thought.

As Beth called time on the constructions, Millie ducked around to the back of the tent and pulled out three pegs, hiding them under the base.

'This looks good,' the camp leader said as she walked around Alice-Miranda and Millie's tent. She tugged at the guide ropes and checked to see that everything was squared off. 'Uh oh,' Beth said from where she was kneeling down at the back. 'You're missing some pegs.' The back half of the construction slowly caved in.

Alice-Miranda frowned at Millie. 'I thought we checked them all.'

Millie nodded. 'Yeah, me too.'

'Sorry, girls, you'll have some points deducted for that,' said Beth as she scribbled on her scoresheet.

Caprice looked over at Millie and smiled. 'Good job, girls.'

The rest of the group had varying degrees of success, from Figgy and Rufus's disaster, which collapsed as soon as Beth crawled inside, to Caprice and Susannah's triumph with a perfect score.

Building a fire was their next task. Although the main fire ring was already in place in the centre of the tents, each child had to build their own smaller version down on the riverbank.

The children spread out and searched for rocks and kindling. Alice-Miranda headed away from the bank to look for some larger branches. While she was gone,

Millie swapped her friend's dry sticks for some green ones she'd just gathered from a nearby willow tree.

Caprice saw exactly what was going on and gave the girl a fairy clap. Millie was a far better helper than she'd ever expected. When Caprice turned away Millie poked out her tongue.

Figgy was hunched over his fire circle rubbing two sticks together. The boy was panting and perspiring.

'What are you doing?' Mr Plumpton asked.

He looked up and took a deep breath. 'Making a fire, sir. I thought that's what we were supposed to do.'

'Yes, but you might like to use these.' Mr Plumpton threw the lad a small box.

'Oh, I didn't realise we could use matches.' Figgy gave a huge sigh of relief.

A pall of white smoke blew all over the campers as Alice-Miranda tried to get her kindling lit.

'Ow! My eyes are stinging,' Jacinta complained, squinting. 'What are you doing, Alice-Miranda? We're not sending smoke signals.'

'Sorry! I thought my twigs were dry,' the child apologised.

'Wonderful, Caprice. Well done,' Beth praised

the girl as her little stack of kindling popped and crackled.

'Rufus, what are you doing?' Mr Plumpton barked. The boy seemed to be building a bonfire worthy of Guy Fawkes. 'Put that timber up near the main fire.'

'Sorry about your fire,' Millie said to Alice-Miranda.

The child shrugged. 'I don't know what's going on with me this afternoon.'

Bile rose in Millie's throat. She hated what she was doing. But after the disaster of the trivia night and Caprice's threats in the canoe, Millie wasn't prepared to take any risks.

Chapter 30

Alice-Miranda snuggled into her sleeping bag and closed her eyes. So far she'd done everything possible to distract herself from thinking about Uncle Ed and the mystery of those paintings. She wondered if that's why she'd made so many mistakes with her camp activities.

The day's final disaster had left her completely mystified. How she'd managed to mix up the sugar and salt when she was making everyone's hot chocolates after dinner, she'd never know. The whole lot had to be thrown out. Caprice then made a batch that was absolutely delicious. Something wasn't right with Millie either, Alice-Miranda thought anxiously. Maybe some fresh air might help.

She felt around for the torch, wriggled out of her downy cocoon then unzipped the tent flap and slid outside. The steady breathing of her fellow campers was punctuated by the odd grunt and snore. She tiptoed past the blackened ring of rocks where the children had toasted marshmallows and told ghost stories several hours before.

The clouds that had released a patter of fat raindrops earlier in the evening had cleared and the sky sparkled with millions of stars. Alice-Miranda could see the distant lights of Pelham Park twinkling in the darkness, and the occasional car on the main road beyond. Their camp site sat almost on the boundary of Pelham Park and Bagley Hall. Rufus was right that it was hardly remote. A road ran parallel to the fence between the two properties less than a hundred metres away. It led down to an ancient stone bridge and up over the rise to the farmhouses and cottages on the Pelham Park estate. Moonlight gleamed on the lake and the pretty stone summer house across the lawn behind the mansion.

A way off down the driveway, Alice-Miranda saw headlights and heard the drone of an engine approaching. It was probably one of the staff heading home after a late evening. A moment later, a van came into view, heading towards the river. Alice-Miranda expected it to keep coming across the bridge and over the hill to the cottages, but it didn't. It turned left and headed towards the summer house.

That was strange. Alice-Miranda decided to take a closer look. She scurried to the fence and clambered over, then darted towards the lake.

As she drew nearer, she heard voices. Two men.

Then she heard the van door slide open.

Alice-Miranda had no idea what they were doing out there in the middle of the night, but something told her that they shouldn't be there. She took cover in the trees.

'Hurry up, Nigel,' one voice whispered.

'I'm coming, Jezza. How about we have a break before we take this one down? It's blinkin' heavy and I've got a nice thermos of tea here. Wife's packed us some pikelets too,' the other man said.

'Ooh, yeah, that'd be nice,' Jezza replied.

Alice-Miranda crept closer and wove her way in and out of the trees until she was within a few metres of the van. Her foot crunched on a stick. The noise echoed in the still night air.

'What was that?' Nigel hissed.

'Nothing,' Jezza replied. 'Probably just a rabbit or something – you're getting jumpy in your old age.'

Alice-Miranda looked at the name on the side of the van. Starchy Brothers Linen Services. If these fellows were delivering the linen for the nursing home, what were they doing parking so far from the house? And why were they working at half past one in the morning?

She dashed behind a tall oak tree and poked her head out. The men were dressed from head to toe in black. That wasn't a good sign.

'Seems like a waste of time taking this one in tonight, given we're about to make a very large withdrawal,' one of the men said.

'Well, we 'ave to put it somewhere in the meantime. And after that close call, when my old lady found the Monet and thought it was her birthday present, this place is safer than my flat. Yours isn't any better – it's like a refuge for delinquent children over there. Besides, it's not our job to ask questions. I'm very 'appy just to get paid,' the other man replied.

'I wonder if the old man's noticed all the additions over the years,' the first gravelly voice said.

'Nah, I heard he was losin' his marbles. Probably just thinks they're his. Anyway, he won't notice anything too much longer.'

'I had wondered how we'd get it all out in one go but Nigel, my friend, you're a genius,' Jezza said. 'That anniversary couldn't have come at a better time.'

'Yes, Mr Goldsworthy's going to be very 'appy with us. There's a lot of interest on that deposit, if you know what I mean,' Nigel said.

Alice-Miranda could hardly believe her ears. *Goldsworthy.* Could it be Addison Goldsworthy? She was sure that Alethea's father was still in prison for tax evasion and a dozen other things. Even behind bars he was up to no good. But who was the old fellow they were talking about?

'I always liked the old boy, you know. Strange one, though. He never sold any of them. Took 'em as payment for work done – I s'pose that's the sort of payment you're likely to get when you represent dodgy blokes like our boss,' the first man said.

'Who you callin' dodgy, Jezza? I'm a very respectable citizen, I am. When I'm not doin' jobs for the likes of Addison Goldsworthy,' Nigel laughed.

'Well, Mr Goldsworthy will be forever in the old bloke's debt for providing the most perfect hiding place. It's just lucky we remembered it when the old fella retired. You finished that tea?'

The other bloke handed his cup over.

'Well, come on then.' Jezza threw the thermos and cups into the van. 'Put your gloves on. Don't want prints on anything.'

A few seconds later, the two men heaved and hauled and eventually pulled out a very large painting. It was at least a metre across and wrapped in a white cloth. Alice-Miranda squinted. The cloth fell to the side, revealing a heavily gilded frame and inside it a portrait of a woman. What were they going to do with it?

The pair strained as they lifted the piece.

'Careful, Jezza,' Nigel said as he repositioned the cloth. 'We'd better not damage her.' They shuffled over to the summer house, opened the door and vanished.

Alice-Miranda was about to follow them when she heard a faint whisper in the darkness. 'Alice-Miranda, where are you?' It was Millie.

She didn't dare call back in case the men reappeared. Alice-Miranda ran as lightly as she could through the trees and to the fence, looking over her shoulder to see if the men had returned.

Nimble as a cat, she hopped up and over, and saw Millie looking towards Pelham Park.

'I'm here,' she whispered.

'Where did you go?'

'I couldn't sleep.' Alice-Miranda looked back towards the summer house, her mind racing.

'Are you okay?' Millie asked.

Alice-Miranda nodded. In the moonlight she could see Millie's eyes were puffy and it looked as if she'd been crying, which was very strange indeed.

'But I was going to ask you the same thing,' Alice-Miranda said.

'I'm okay,' Millie said.

'That's not true. I know you,' Alice-Miranda said seriously. 'We're best friends, remember? I've had a strange feeling that something hasn't been right for the past couple of days. Have you been crying?'

Millie couldn't keep Caprice's evil blackmail to herself any longer. 'You're not going to want to be my friend when you hear this. But you have to promise not to do anything and you can't tell the teachers.' Millie's face crumpled.

'What's the matter? What are you talking about?' Alice-Miranda reached out and squeezed Millie's hand.

Fat tears rolled down the girl's cheeks. She brushed them away. 'Promise you won't hate me,' Millie begged.

'I could never hate you,' Alice-Miranda said.

Millie took a deep breath. 'Caprice said that if I didn't do everything she told me to, you would get hurt.'

'What? That's ridiculous.' Alice-Miranda shook her head.

'You don't understand. She's crazy. She said that she had to leave her last school because she pushed a girl down the stairs,' Millie sobbed.

Alice-Miranda put her arm around Millie's shoulder. 'That's terrible. But you should have told me.'

'The accident at archery. She meant for that to happen. She told me next time things would get messy. I was terrified that she would do something awful – or worse, set me up to do it.' Millie fished around in her sleeve and pulled out a tissue.

'I knew there was something wrong. Millie, we're a team. We would have figured it out,'

Alice-Miranda said. 'So I didn't really mix up the sugar and the salt?'

Millie shook her head.

'And I wasn't going mad when I thought I'd put those tent pegs in?'

'No, that was all me.'

'But the fire?'

Millie sniffed. 'I swapped your dry sticks for green ones. Are you angry?'

'Of course not. You were only trying to protect me.' The two girls hugged each other tightly. 'Don't worry about Caprice. We can deal with her later. But I have something to tell you too.'

Millie wiped her face. 'What's the matter?'

'You know Uncle Ed has come to sort out Granny's art collection?'

Millie nodded.

'Well, this morning he took me downstairs to have a look and we discovered something very strange,' the child began.

'What was it?' Millie asked.

'One of the paintings I saw was *stolen*,' Alice-Miranda whispered. 'Uncle Ed said that it wasn't the only one. Detective Freeman was with us, but I don't think she saw anything.'

'But shouldn't you tell her?' asked Millie.

'That's what I said, but Uncle Ed wants to go through the rest of the collection first,' Alice-Miranda replied.

'Your grandfather was rich. It's not as if he would have needed to steal art.' Millie chewed her pinkie nail as she thought it through.

'That's the thing. The painting I saw was stolen only a few years ago. It couldn't have been Grandpa at all. He's been dead for more than twenty years.'

'Then who?' Millie asked. 'Could it be someone in the house?'

'I don't know. But I just saw the strangest thing.' Alice-Miranda told Millie all about the two men and the van and what they had said about making a withdrawal. She was afraid they were planning to steal all of the paintings.

Millie's eyes widened. 'You don't think your uncle could believe that your parents are responsible, do you?'

'I don't know what he's thinking but I need to get back to the house and find out what else he's discovered as soon as possible. Mummy and Daddy are away until Saturday morning and then they're coming to the fair. I just hope Uncle Ed gets to the bottom of things before then,' Alice-Miranda said breathlessly.

Alice-Miranda and Millie weren't the only campers awake. Caprice had hopped up to go to the toilet. As the girl was about to return to bed, she thought she heard voices in the distance. When she had realised it was Millie and Alice-Miranda, she had sneaked over and crouched down behind a tree.

Millie held Alice-Miranda's hand. 'I'm glad everything's okay with us.'

Alice-Miranda smiled. 'Me too.'

Caprice could feel her heart pounding. That little brat Millie had better not have said anything – or else.

Chapter 31

Friday dawned bright and clear. Ed Clifton jolted awake and rolled over to look at the clock beside the bed. It was just after seven. He'd only had a few hours' sleep as his mind had been racing all night. He had replayed the discoveries he'd made downstairs, and kept wondering 'how?' and even more urgently 'who?'.

Of the sixty-eight paintings he'd examined and catalogued, five were stolen. He wasn't even halfway through the collection, which made him wonder what other surprises were in store. Three of the missing works had disappeared more than thirty years ago but two had come from much more recent thefts. As far as Ed understood, only he and his brother knew the combination for the vault.

Ed pushed back the covers, stretched and then headed into the bathroom. His breakfast tray was waiting for him when he came out of the shower. He found it slightly unnerving that someone had a key to his room and was happy to let themselves in. He hoped it was only the matron. It got him thinking about keys – Matron Bright had mentioned that she'd lost a set when Pelham Park first opened.

Ed opened the door and almost bumped into Matron Bright.

'Good morning, Mr Clifton,' she sang.

Ed nodded. 'Good morning, matron. Thanks for breakfast.'

'My pleasure. I suppose you're off to the cellars now?' the woman said.

'Yes, I'll be there all day. I hadn't realised Mother had such an extensive collection. When Alice-Miranda's group arrives today, would you bring her downstairs? She was very helpful yesterday and I could do with another pair of hands.'

'Oh yes, of course, so long as it's all right with Mr Plumpton. I don't imagine he'll mind.'

'Thanks.' Ed grinned tightly. 'If you could just let her through the locked doors. I know she'll find her way from there.'

'Certainly, Mr Clifton.' She took a large key out of her pocket and unlocked the door to Ed's room. 'I'll just take your tray.'

Ed almost flew downstairs. As he opened the vault door and looked about, his head began to spin and he thought he might lose his breakfast.

'How on earth?' he breathed. Before him was a painting he certainly hadn't seen the day before. He recognised it immediately. How could he not? It had been stolen from The Met a couple of months ago. He knew all about it, because it was one of his own.

Mr Plumpton yawned as he emerged from his tent. He looked as if he'd fought ten rounds with a tiger. His shirt buttons were mismatched and his trousers crumpled.

The children were all up and engaged in various jobs. Several had gone to collect kindling for the fire and others were down by the creek washing their faces. The shovel had disappeared too.

'Good morning, Mr Plumpton,' Alice-Miranda greeted the teacher.

'Good morning to you too, young lady. Did you sleep well?'

'Not especially.'

'Me neither,' Mr Plumpton confided. 'I'll be glad to be in a bed again tonight. I really don't think my old bones are cut out for camping.'

'Mr Plumpton, you're not that old,' Alice-Miranda said with a grin. 'Do you know what time we're going to Pelham Park today?'

'Hang on a tick.' The teacher consulted the revised timetable that Miss Reedy had given him the day before. 'It looks like you're due over there at ten, then back to Bagley Hall early in the afternoon for an extended choir practice with Mr Lipp.'

Mr Plumpton was very pleased that his entire group belonged to the Winchester-Fayle Singers. He was looking forward to a cup of tea and a nap while the children rehearsed.

'Thank you, sir,' Alice-Miranda replied.

It didn't take long for the children to eat breakfast and get the camp site packed up. Millie groaned when Beth told the children that the paddling groups were to stay the same as the day before. Her arms ached at the thought of it.

'Isn't it lovely to be together again?' Caprice asked, smiling at her two companions.

'Do you think you could help us paddle this time?' Millie grumbled.

'I paddled yesterday,' Caprice bit, then turned and smiled at Figgy.

He was more gaga over the girl than ever and leapt to her defence. 'Millie, leave her alone. She was paddling every time I looked.'

'You're so blind, Figgy. She was sitting behind you and only paddling when you turned around.' Millie shook her head and stomped over to load the canoe. She didn't notice Caprice following her.

'Have you forgotten our deal?'

Millie whirled around to face her. 'No, of course not.'

'I'm going to win that medal,' Caprice whispered, her eyes narrowed.

'Won't that feel good?' Millie said. 'Knowing that you've made your competition look bad. You make me sick!'

'Aren't we brave all of a sudden?' Caprice hissed. 'I hope you haven't forgotten our little arrangement.'

Millie sighed. 'I don't know how you sleep at night.'

'Maybe I don't.' Caprice raised her eyebrows. 'You never know what sort of things you might hear in the woods after midnight.'

Millie gulped. Could Caprice have overheard her and Alice-Miranda talking?

The return trip along the river was much faster than their extended journey out. Before they knew it, they'd rounded the bend and were back at home base. It was just after nine thirty.

'Okay, everyone. You've got ten minutes to put your sleeping bags and clothes back in your rooms and brush your teeth,' Beth instructed.

The Barn Owls scattered. Mr Plumpton walked into the teacher's lounge to deposit his things and make a quick cup of tea.

Miss Reedy looked up from where she was sorting through a pile of paperwork. 'Good morning, Josiah. How was your camp-out?'

'Hello Livinia. It was no more exciting than I had anticipated, although a few of the children surprised me.' He walked to the sink and filled the kettle. 'Would you like tea?'

'I'm fine for now. Which children?' asked Miss Reedy.

'For a start, Rufus Pemberley has a future as a pyromaniac. You should have seen the size of the fire he was building.'

Miss Reedy grinned and shook her head. 'Who else made an impression?'

'Sep Sykes – he's a star, that lad. And Caprice was outstanding too but I was surprised at Alice-Miranda. She made quite a hash of things yesterday. That's not like her at all,' Mr Plumpton said with a frown.

'You know, we do place very high expectations on her. Nobody's perfect,' Miss Reedy replied.

'Yes, you're right, but this is Alice-Miranda we're talking about. I just can't shake the feeling that there's more to it.'

Chapter 32

Fenella Freeman had hardly slept a wink. The murder she had gone to investigate was indeed grizzly, but thankfully the victims were not human: foxes had got into Mrs Playfair's chicken coop and the woman was hysterical. Fenella had eventually returned to the station and spent several hours researching the stolen Turner. By the time she'd headed home she was absolutely sure that Hugh Kennington-Jones was in possession of a very valuable painting that didn't belong to him.

Today was a turning point. A major bust like this would change everything. She'd secured a search warrant as soon as the magistrate had arrived at the courthouse, then driven to Pelham Park just after nine thirty. Matron Bright had been happy to take her straight to the cellars, although the woman hardly seemed to register when Fenella informed her that she was on official police business. She seemed much more concerned with the whereabouts of her missing shortbread order for the fair. Fenella was delighted to find Ed Clifton and his brother in the vault.

She looked around at the artworks and then back at Ed. Nothing they had told her made any sense at all. 'Seriously, this just keeps getting better and better,' she scoffed. 'You had your own painting stolen from The Met and put it here with all the other stolen art.'

Hugh shook his head. 'The stolen paintings are not ours. It's as much a mystery to us as it is to you.'

Ed had telephoned Hugh as soon as he'd discovered his own painting newly arrived in the vault. Hugh had literally flown over from Highton Hall in Birdy, the family chopper.

'I don't know why people like you always think you're going to get away with it,' Fenella said bitterly.

‘We’re not trying to get away with anything,’ Ed retorted. ‘You’re leaping to conclusions.’

‘I don’t think so. There’s quite a bit of evidence right here.’ She picked up Ed’s inventory and flicked through the pages. ‘So, the ones you’ve marked with an asterisk – are those also stolen?’

‘Detective Freeman, if I was trying to hide anything, why would I scribble all over that sheet questioning everything?’

‘I don’t expect you ever thought I’d find it,’ she said. ‘And it was pretty clever of you too, bringing me down here yesterday. Did you think I was just some hick policewoman without a worldly bone in her body? I don’t suppose you thought I knew anything about art. You’re wrong. I know plenty and my father is an expert.’

‘Bring in your teams. Do the forensics,’ said Hugh. ‘We’ve got nothing to hide. Ed was planning to go to the police as soon as he’d worked out exactly how much of it was stolen.’

‘Don’t you worry. This place will be searched from top to bottom. But for now, I’m arresting both of you for possession of stolen goods,’ Fenella said.

Hugh exploded. ‘Arresting us! You can’t do that. We haven’t done anything wrong!’

But Fenella Freeman didn't see it that way. These two could spend the night in the lockup and that would give her free rein to do a proper search of the house.

'Come on, then,' she ordered.

'No,' Hugh retorted. 'I'm not going anywhere!'

'Would you like me to add resisting arrest to the charge sheet?' Fenella threatened.

'Let's just go with her, Hugh. We can phone Cee from the station and sort something out,' Ed urged.

'That's a very sensible approach, Mr Clifton.' Fenella smiled smugly and pulled a pair of shiny silver handcuffs from her belt.

Hugh's jaw dropped. 'You're not serious.'

'I won't make you wear them as long as you come willingly,' the detective said.

'Mr Plumpton, may I go and help Uncle Ed this morning?' Alice-Miranda asked as the Barn Owls trotted up the driveway to Pelham Park. She was walking beside Millie and the teacher at the back of the group.

'I don't see why not, as long as it's all right with Matron Bright,' he replied.

The children were entering the house just as a police car drove around from the back of the building. Detective Freeman certainly spent a lot of time visiting her father, Alice-Miranda thought to herself.

Millie tugged on Alice-Miranda's sleeve and pointed. 'Is that your father? In the back of the police car?'

Alice-Miranda glimpsed two heads through the windscreen. Her stomach lurched. She had a horrible feeling it was her father in there, and that Uncle Ed was with him. She needed to get down to the cellar as quickly as possible.

Chapter 33

'Uncle Ed, are you down here?' Alice-Miranda called as she wove her way through the maze of furniture. Millie was right behind her.

The girl marvelled at the strange display and shuddered at all the stuffed animals. 'It's like an antique shop. A really freaky one.'

Matron Bright had grabbed Alice-Miranda as soon as she arrived and explained that her father had turned up at the house very early that morning and gone to the cellar with her uncle. Detective Freeman had arrived about an hour ago and requested access down there too. The matron hadn't seen the three of them emerge and believed that they were all still downstairs.

The rest of the Barn Owls were directed to jobs for the fair, but Millie had rushed off with Alice-Miranda. The girls reached the vault but the door was closed.

'I told you I saw them in the police car. You don't think they could have been arrested, do you?' asked Millie.

'Of course not,' said Alice-Miranda, but she wasn't really sure.

Millie pointed at the door. 'Do you know the combination?

Alice-Miranda stared at the dial. She shook her head.

'Try four, three, two, one,' Millie suggested.

Alice-Miranda spun the dial but the door remained firmly shut.

'Maybe the other way around,' Millie said.

'I think that's too obvious,' Alice-Miranda said. 'Maybe it's someone's birthday? I'll try Daddy's.'

It was another dead end.

'What about the year this place was founded?' Millie said. 'That could make sense.'

Alice-Miranda nodded. 'Tomorrow the house is one hundred and fifty years old so that would make the foundation date . . . 1864,' Alice-Miranda counted off the clicks.

There was a clank as the bolts slid back.

'You did it!' Millie beamed. Alice-Miranda grabbed the handle. Millie did too, and together the girls pulled the heavy door open.

'Whoa!' Millie said as she spied the underground art gallery.

Alice-Miranda drew in a sharp breath. 'Oh my goodness! That's it! It's the painting I saw last night.'

'With the men, in the van?' Millie said. 'But how did it get in here?'

'I don't know.' Alice-Miranda thought about it. 'There must be passage from the summer house.'

Millie scanned the walls, searching for something to indicate a doorway.

Alice-Miranda studied the recent addition carefully and looked at the signature in the bottom right-hand corner.

'I can't believe this,' she gasped.

Millie was busily running her hands over the bare bricks. 'What are you talking about?' She ran back to where Alice-Miranda was kneeling in front of the portrait.

'The artist. It's Uncle Ed,' she said.

'That's ridiculous. Has anything of his been stolen?' Millie asked.

Alice-Miranda nodded. Her parents had told her about a theft at The Metropolitan Museum in New York a couple of months ago. One of Uncle Ed's paintings was among several works that had gone missing. But how did it end up here?

'We need to find that passageway,' Millie said.

Alice-Miranda nodded. 'I've got an idea. If anyone's going to know about secret passageways, it's Mr Freeman.'

She grabbed Millie's hand and together the girls raced upstairs, leaving the doors open in their wake. They charged up the back staircase to the first floor and ran along the hall. Fortunately, the apartments each had the name of the resident on a plaque on the door.

Alice-Miranda found Mr Freeman's name, knocked loudly and then waited, jiggling up and down impatiently with Millie beside her. 'Mr Freeman, are you there?' she called after a few moments.

There was a shuffling sound on the other side of the door.

'Mr Freeman, I need to ask you a question. It's very important.'

She heard the lock turn and the door opened. Alice-Miranda barged inside with Millie behind her.

Donald mumbled, 'What's the matter? What's this all about?'

'Mr Freeman, I can't remember if I told you earlier in the week that Uncle Ed is here cataloguing Granny's art collection so that it can be sold,' she began to explain. 'Well, we've discovered some very odd things down there and I need to ask you a question.'

Donald sat in his armchair heavily, jolting a little crystal bowl of gold-wrapped chocolates on the table beside him.

Millie looked towards the noise.

'Have one,' the old man offered.

But neither girl was in the mood for sweets. 'No, thank you,' said Alice-Miranda. Millie shook her head.

'Mr Freeman, the other day, you said that you and Harry could get into the house without anyone knowing. How did you do it?'

'I told you it doesn't matter,' Donald muttered.

'But it does. I think my father and Uncle Ed are in big trouble and I need to know. Your daughter was driving them away in her police car when we got here. Last night I saw some men near the summer house. They were carrying a painting and then they disappeared.'

Donald Freeman looked as if the wind had been sucked out of his sails.

'What men?'

'One was called Jezza and the other was Nigel,' Alice-Miranda replied.

'Don't be ridiculous!' Mr Freeman snapped.

'Is there a secret passageway to the cellars?' Alice-Miranda begged. 'Please. I have to know.'

'No! Now off you go, the pair of you, before I call the matron,' Donald stood up and ushered the girls out the door.

Chapter 34

'There you are, girls.' Matron Bright hurried towards Alice-Miranda and Millie. 'Mr Plumpton's been looking for you. Beth's taken the rest of the Barn Owls back to school for lunch and choir practice and I gather you two are not going to be in the good books.'

'Where is he now?' Millie asked.

'Right here,' Josiah Plumpton blustered as he turned the corner. Beads of perspiration peppered his brow and he was aware of two wet patches under his arms. He'd been up and down searching for Millie, who should have been helping in the kitchen. He knew that Alice-Miranda was with her uncle and had planned to send for her once he located everyone else. 'Where have you been, Millicent? No one has seen you all morning and now you're both late for choir practice.'

Millie looked at the floor. 'Sorry, Mr Plumpton. I . . . I was . . .'

'She was helping me,' Alice-Miranda said. 'Uncle Ed needed us to carry some things upstairs for him.'

'It would have been useful for you to tell me that,' the man sighed.

'Sorry, Mr Plumpton, I knew Millie was with Alice-Miranda but I'm afraid I have a thousand things on my mind. That reminds me. Are your father and uncle still downstairs, Alice-Miranda?' Matron Bright asked. She really didn't have time today to be chasing the Kennington-Jones men. There were stalls being set up outside and rides about to be delivered too. Tomorrow's fair was Dunleavy's biggest event of the year.

'Yes,' said Alice-Miranda. 'They're very busy.'

Millie glanced at her friend and wondered what she was playing at.

The matron nodded. 'That's fine, as long as they keep out of my way this afternoon. Oh look, here are some more helpers now.'

One of the camp leaders had just arrived in the foyer with two groups of students ready for the afternoon shift.

'Hello there, my lovelies,' Matron Bright beamed. 'Have I got some jobs for you!'

'Come along, girls. We need to get back to camp before Mr Lipp blows a gasket,' said Mr Plumpton. He hurried away, with Alice-Miranda and Millie racing to catch up.

'How nice of you girls to join us,' said Mr Lipp, giving Alice-Miranda and Millie a frosty glare as they arrived. Mr Plumpton had taken the girls via the dining room to grab a sandwich on their way. He didn't think another ten minutes could make Mr Lipp's mood any worse and he was right about that. 'I thought this award you're striving for is all about being in the right place at the right time?'

'Sorry we're late, Mr Lipp,' said Alice-Miranda.

'Fine. We'll take it from the top. Caprice, are you ready, my dear?'

The girl smiled sweetly. She was pleased to see that Millie was still doing her job properly. After the number of things Alice-Miranda had messed up in the past twenty-four hours, the brat couldn't possibly be in the running for the Queen's Medal now.

Mr Lipp held his hands aloft and snapped his fingers to count Mr Trout in on the piano.

Choir practice stretched on forever. By the time Mr Lipp had finished with the children it was almost dinner.

Alice-Miranda and Millie were on their way to the dining room when they were intercepted by Miss Reedy.

'Alice-Miranda, may I have a quick word?' the teacher asked.

The girl turned to Millie. 'I'll meet you inside.'

'I've just had a very odd message,' Miss Reedy said. 'Is everything all right?'

'What do you mean, Miss Reedy?'

'Well, Mrs Oliver called from Highton Hall and asked me to tell you that your father and Uncle Ed had gone away for the night. They'll be back tomorrow and all is well,' Miss Reedy said. 'I have no idea what she was talking about, nor why you would even be concerned. I'm assuming that there is something going on that you need to tell me about.'

Alice-Miranda shook her head. 'Uncle Ed is staying at Pelham Park at the moment. If he and Daddy have gone somewhere for the night, I suppose they just wanted to let me know in case I was looking for him.' She had been thinking about telling Miss Reedy the truth but the teacher would want to call the police. Alice-Miranda didn't want to involve the police until she had some proof about those two men in the van.

'Oh. Well, that does sound like a sensible explanation,' said Miss Reedy. 'But seriously, Alice-Miranda, are you all right? Mr Plumpton mentioned that you hadn't done as well as he had hoped with some of your challenges, which is not like you at all.' The teacher looked at her intently.

'I'm sorry, Miss Reedy. Things were just trickier than I was ready for, I suppose,' the child said with a shrug.

Miss Reedy wasn't buying it. There was something else going on in that clever head of Alice-Miranda's.

'Sweetheart, you would tell me if there was something wrong?' Miss Reedy bit her lip.

The child nodded. She wanted to, but not yet.

Miss Reedy suppressed a sigh. 'Well, run along.'

Millie waved to Alice-Miranda from a table in the far corner. 'What did she say?'

'Mrs Oliver called and left a message that Daddy and Uncle Ed had gone away for the night and I wasn't to worry. I'm glad they managed to speak to her.'

'Mrs Oliver is so clever. "Gone away" is much better than saying they'd been arrested,' Millie said.

'Millie!' Alice-Miranda stared at her friend and pressed her finger against her lip.

She grimaced. 'Sorry. What are you going to do?'

Alice-Miranda shrugged. Her mind was in a whirl.

After dinner, Miss Reedy announced that there would be a short round of games in the gym followed by an early night. They all had to be next door by half past eight the next morning to help with the fair.

The camp leaders briefed their groups about the stalls they'd be helping on and the elderly residents they'd be assisting. Caprice, Sloane and Jacinta were posted to the second-hand bookshop, while Sep and Lucas were manning the jumping castle.

'That's not fair,' Sloane griped. 'Why do they get to have all the fun and we have to look after a bunch of dusty old books?'

'They're not allowed *on* the jumping castle,' said Mr Plumpton. 'They're taking money and making sure the littlies are playing safely.'

Sloane nodded. 'That's okay then.'

Alice-Miranda, Millie, Rufus and Figgy would each accompany an elderly resident around the fair.

'Seriously, sir, do I have to?' Figgy complained. 'He's just going to whinge all day.'

'What, like you are now?' the teacher quipped.

Susannah had managed to get herself a job as a waitress in the tea marquee.

'I hope Mr Freeman's in a better mood than he was this morning,' Millie whispered to Alice-Miranda.

Alice-Miranda hoped so too.

Chapter 35

Alice-Miranda was awake and dressed before dawn. She'd hardly slept thinking about what was going on at Pelham Park and wondering how her father and Uncle Ed were.

'Good morning, everyone,' cried Mr Lipp as the children traipsed into the dining room for breakfast.

Figgy shielded his face and took a step back. 'My eyes, my eyes!'

'What's the matter, Figworth?' asked Mr Lipp.

'Your suit, sir. It's blinding me.'

Harry Lipp had outdone himself this morning in a silky lime green ensemble with a bright pink shirt and a blue spotted tie.

He glared at the lad. 'One day, Figworth, I hope you will appreciate high fashion.'

'Loud fashion did you say, sir?' the boy called before scuttling away to the servery.

Just before the children left for Pelham Park, Miss Reedy announced the group points tally. Sure enough, another of the groups that hadn't previously won anything was now in the lead.

'See, I told you this thing was rigged,' Sloane said. 'The Barn Owls have to win sometime between now and tomorrow morning, or we are seriously a bunch of losers.'

'Who are you calling a loser?' Caprice sneered.

'Us,' said Sloane. 'We haven't won anything.'

'*You* might not have . . .' Caprice said smugly.

Miss Reedy continued her announcements. 'Quite a number of children have consistently impressed the teachers and are in the running for the Queen's Medal, but there is one stand-out at the moment.'

Caprice was waiting for the teacher to announce the names, certain that her own would be on the list.

But Miss Reedy simply said that she would keep the children guessing.

Miss Reedy had taken a phone call from Miss Grimm late the previous evening. She was stunned when the headmistress announced that she would be visiting the fair with Queen Georgiana and they wanted a full briefing before Her Majesty would announce the recipients of the Blues and the winner of the Medal at exactly 1 pm. Her Majesty had decided that as she'd been invited to the Pelham Park Fair anyway, she might as well kill two birds with one stone.

Kill Miss Reedy was more like it, the teacher thought. She had spent half the night calculating scores and checking which of the children had earned their Blues. To say that the results had surprised her was something of an understatement.

'All right, everyone. Be on your best behaviour, please. There is still time to earn the extra points some of you need to achieve your Blue,' Miss Reedy explained. She was armed with her clipboard and score sheet and ready for action.

It was just after eight thirty when the children arrived at Pelham Park. The fair was due to commence at nine and there was a lot to do before then.

Matron Bright looked as happy and unflustered as ever and seemed genuinely grateful for the hordes of helpers. The children walked around to the back of the house and found the lawns transformed by rows of stalls, a roped-off area with rides and a jumping castle, and a huge marquee in the middle where someone was testing a PA system.

'For those of you looking after a resident, wheelchairs will be available. It will be a tiring day for them, so please don't walk too fast, and make sure you stop for regular food and toot breaks,' Matron Bright explained. 'I've asked the residents to meet us in the Great Hall at nine o'clock. In the meantime, you can help me to finish setting up the tea marquee. The rest of you, please report to your stations.'

The children scattered all over the place.

Alice-Miranda and Millie ran around putting cloths on the tables in the tea marquee. 'I wish I knew what was happening with Daddy and Uncle Ed,' Alice-Miranda told Millie quietly.

'Surely they'll be out on bail soon,' Millie said. She'd watched quite a few detective shows with her mother in the holidays. 'It's not like they're murderers.'

Alice-Miranda frowned. 'No, just multimillion dollar art thieves, according to Detective Freeman.'

Matron Bright surveyed the tent.

'Well done, everyone. Figgy and Rufus, your flower arranging is superb,' she said, beaming. 'I will be passing that on to Miss Reedy.'

The lads grinned. They'd been less than impressed when assigned the task of filling fifty vases with flowers but it turned out that the pair had an eye for floristry.

'Let's go and round everyone up.' Matron Bright wiped her hands on her apron and set off for the house with the children behind her.

There was much excitement inside among the residents.

'Hello Millie,' Mrs Von Thripp greeted the child. 'Did you see any craft stalls out there? I need a new door snake and I thought you might be able to carry it for me – they weigh a tonne with all that sand.'

Figgy and Rufus offered Mr Mobbs and Mr Johnson wheelchairs and were very pleased when the men agreed. The boys grinned – this was going to be much more fun than they'd thought.

'Matron, do you know where Mr Freeman is?' Alice-Miranda asked, having skirted the foyer and poked her head into both the reading and games rooms.

'He must be running late,' the woman said. 'Why don't you pop up and see if he's home?'

Alice-Miranda dashed up the stairs two at a time. She rang the buzzer on his door and waited. 'Hello Mr Freeman, are you coming to the fair?' she called.

The door opened and Donald Freeman poked his head outside.

'I'm supposed to be accompanying you to the fair, Mr Freeman,' the child said. 'I'm sorry to have upset you yesterday.'

The man stared at her blankly.

'You were cross because I asked how you and Harry used to come and go to the house unnoticed,' she reminded him.

'Oh, did you? Is your father back?' he said.

Alice-Miranda wondered how it was that he could remember some things so clearly while others seemed to pass him by. 'No. He and Uncle Ed are still away,' she explained. 'I'm sure Mummy must be with them now though.'

'Then I'd rather not come out,' the man said.

'Oh, I'm sorry to hear that,' said Alice-Miranda. She'd hoped that if she spent some time with the man, he might open up a bit. 'If you change your mind, I'll be outside.'

Donald Freeman closed the door and paced the room. He had to get back downstairs. He'd thought he'd be able to get it done last night but the frames were far too heavy. When he'd come back upstairs to get the knife he'd fallen asleep. He was confused too. There were things that didn't belong. But he was certain that those men shouldn't have to pay for something their father did so long ago.

Alice-Miranda walked around the balcony to the main stairs. She bounced down and across the Great Hall on her way to the back entrance.

Mr Freeman was a complicated fellow. And not well either, she was quite sure of it. She sniffled and pulled a tissue from her jeans pocket. A shiny gold wrapper fluttered to the floor. Alice-Miranda reached down to pick it up. She'd found it in the vault and forgotten that she'd stuffed it in her pocket.

'Oh!' She clutched her hands to her mouth. 'I know where that came from.' She turned back towards the stairs and glimpsed someone rounding the corner of the upstairs corridor. They were heading towards the back stairs. Alice-Miranda took off. What was really going on?

Chapter 36

Millie could hardly believe the shopping stamina of Mrs Von Thripp. The woman purchased the heaviest door snake she could find – in the shape of a sausage dog – and had also bought herself a new tea cosy, a cover for the toaster and half-a-dozen placemats.

As the pair turned the corner near the second-hand book stall, the old woman's eyes lit up.

'Look, Millie! Isn't this wonderful? I'd like to buy at least a dozen books,' she chortled. 'And I don't believe in paperbacks.'

Millie sighed. Her arms still hadn't recovered from the canoeing expedition and now they were just about falling off under the weight of the shopping, without adding a pile of books. She looked about and saw one of the spare wheelchairs. Millie raced off to get it and dumped Mrs Von Thripp's purchases on the seat. She pushed it back to the book stall as fast as she could.

The woman clasped her hands together in delight. 'What a thoughtful girl you are.'

Millie looked at her in confusion and then heaved another sigh. She picked up the pile and looked for somewhere to attach the bags. Mrs Von Thripp hopped into the contraption and waited for Millie to push her.

'Now, dear, you'll have to carry my parcels or it will make the chair unstable,' the old woman instructed.

'Very thoughtful of you, Millie,' said Miss Reedy as she walked past. 'You might just earn that Blue yet.'

'Really?' Millie grinned tightly.

'Have you seen Alice-Miranda and Mr Freeman?' Miss Reedy asked.

Millie shook her head. She'd been keeping an eye out but they were nowhere to be found.

'Well, enjoy your morning, and don't forget the choir's first performance is at midday.' With that Miss Reedy sauntered over to the book stall to talk to Sloane, Jacinta and Caprice.

Mr Plumpton had been wandering about and observing the children's work too. He spotted Figgy and Rufus, who were both pushing wheelchairs.

He nodded. 'Very considerate.' Then he realised exactly what the boys were up to.

'On your marks, get set, GO!' Figgy shouted. The two lads started slowly but were building to a run.

'Woohoo!' Mr Mobbs shouted and pumped the air with his fist.

Mr Johnson leaned forward in his chair. 'Come on, boy, let's beat that old buzzard!'

The lads were flying down the driveway towards the overflow car park.

'Stop!' the teacher shouted. He took off after them as fast as his little legs could carry him. 'Stop now or you'll kill someone.'

'We won!' Mr Mobbs clapped loudly. 'Well done, boy.'

'I demand a rematch.' Mr Johnson's smile was wider than a whale's.

Mr Plumpton caught up to the foursome, puffing and wheezing. 'Good heavens, what on earth do you boys think you were doing? You could have killed these two gentlemen.'

'It was their idea,' Figgy retorted.

'Surely not,' Mr Plumpton replied. 'You lads should know better.'

Mr Mobbs and Mr Johnson glared at the teacher. 'Leave those lads alone,' Mr Mobbs demanded. 'That's the most fun I've had in years. Come on, then. Let's do it again.'

'But, gentlemen, I must insist . . .' Mr Plumpton began.

'There's more chance of you having a heart attack, tubby, than of those boys doing us an injury,' Mr Johnson quipped.

'Suit yourselves. But don't come running to me when there's blood.' Mr Plumpton took a deep breath and stalked off towards the tea marquee. He could do with a brew and a cheese scone.

'Would you like a cup of tea, Mrs Von Thripp?' Millie asked. She was hoping to leave her in the tent for a few minutes and look for Alice-Miranda.

'Oh yes, dear, that would be marvellous.'

Millie pushed her into the tea marquee, where

Mr Lipp and Mr Trout were busy setting up the stage for the choir's performance.

Millie found a table and quickly organised some tea and scones.

'I've, uh . . . just got to go to the toilet,' the child fibbed. She ran out of the marquee and looked down towards the summer house. There were several large trucks parked close to it, obscuring her view.

What Millie saw next set her eyes agog. It was a man carrying a painting. He disappeared into the back of one of the trucks.

She had to find Alice-Miranda. It was today. Jezza and Nigel were clearing out the cellar *today*. In broad daylight, in the middle of the fair. The hide of them.

Millie raced back towards the marquee. She almost bumped into Jacinta and Sloane, who were taking a quick break.

'What's the matter?' Jacinta said. 'You look as if you've seen a ghost.'

'I need to find Alice-Miranda,' Millie gasped.

'Why? What's wrong?' Sloane demanded.

Sep and Lucas had been relieved of their post at the jumping castle for a few minutes and saw the girls together.

'Having fun?' Sep asked.

Millie ignored him and glanced back towards the lake. What if she couldn't find Alice-Miranda before the crooks left?

'What's wrong with you, Millie?' asked Lucas.

'We need to do something,' she said. She hoped that Alice-Miranda hadn't seen the criminals first, and tried to go after them on her own.

'What are you talking about?' Sloane huffed.

'I think Alice-Miranda might be in trouble,' said Millie. 'Her father and uncle have been arrested.'

'What?' The kids were incredulous.

'When and how?' Lucas asked. 'And why didn't we know about this?'

Before Millie could explain, there was a burst of crackle from the PA system.

'Good morning, everyone. What a fine day it is,' blared Mr Lipp's voice.

'Turn it down, sunshine, we're not deaf, you know,' an elderly gentleman in the tent complained, rubbing his finger in his ear.

Mr Lipp cleared his throat. 'Huhhrmm. I wanted to remind everyone that in just over half an hour's time the Winchester-Fayle Singers, for whom I am the choirmaster, will be performing a medley of songs right here in the tea marquee. That's also a reminder to the students that I will be expecting them for a little warm-up in ten minutes' time.'

'Ten minutes,' Millie said. 'We can't wait until after we sing. The thieves will be gone by then and there'll be no proof that it wasn't Hugh and Ed who masterminded the whole thing.'

'What should we do?' Lucas asked.

'We've got to catch them in the act,' Millie said defiantly.

'Okay,' said Sep. 'Let's go down there and see what we can find out.'

Caprice walked into the marquee just as the five friends were heading towards the lake. 'Where are they going?' she mumbled to herself.

'Excuse me, dear? Have you seen Millie?' Mrs Von Thripp asked.

Caprice noticed Mr Plumpton sitting at a table nearby.

'Oh, I'm sorry but I think she's gone to play with her friends,' Caprice said loudly. 'But I can help you.' She smiled sweetly at the old woman.

Mr Plumpton wondered what Caprice was talking about. Millie knew that she was to remain with her resident. This wasn't meant to be a day off.

Chapter 37

Alice-Miranda followed Mr Freeman through the kitchen into the butler's pantry. She hoped that he hadn't locked the door and she was in luck. She waited until she couldn't see any torchlight and then tiptoed down the stairs. When she reached the bottom she pushed open the second door and slipped in among the bric-a-brac, treading a soft path to the vault.

Outside, Millie whispered what she knew about the stolen art and Hugh and Ed's arrest to the other children as they scurried towards the summer house.

They found a good vantage point to observe the building, and crouched behind some trees.

Two men went between the summer house and one of the trucks, loading a new painting into the truck each time. Each new deposit was stacked into a rack and covered with a blanket. They had a routine going, with one man heading in and the other heading out, so that the truck was manned at all times.

'All right, Nigel, that's nearly the last of the small stuff. I'll need a hand with the next one,' one of the men said to the other as they passed each other near the summer house door. They didn't see the children crouched behind the trees just a few metres away.

'I've got an idea,' Sep whispered.

The children listened to his plan.

'I think you're mad, but it might just work,' Lucas said with a grin.

The PA system crackled again.

'Could all of the Winchester-Fayle Singers please join me in the tea marquee now?' requested Mr Lipp testily.

The children looked at each other.

'He'll just have to make do without us,' Jacinta said. 'I'm not leaving you guys to do this on your own.'

The children huddled together.

'Are we ready?' Sep whispered.

The rest of the group nodded. 'Ready.'

Sep and Lucas waited until the man walked up the ramp and into the truck to deposit another painting. Millie gave the nod and the boys unhooked the doors and swung them closed as quickly as they could.

'Hey!' What's going on!' the man demanded. 'Jezza, are you out there? What are you doing? I can't see anything. Help! Let me out of here!'

Lucas and Sep held the doors while Jacinta and Sloane pulled the pins down and locked them into place.

Millie snapped closed the padlock that had been left dangling on the door.

'Come on, let's go,' said Lucas. He held the door open to the summer house. At the back of the building was an open trapdoor. It led down into a tunnel that must have run the length of the lawn to the house.

Back at the tea marquee, Mr Lipp's voice burbled through the PA system once more. 'Sep, Lucas,

Jacinta, Millie, Sloane and Alice-Miranda, make your way to the tea marquee immediately. We are waiting for you.'

'Caprice, did you see where they went?' Mr Plumpton asked the girl, who was standing front and centre on the makeshift stage.

'Yes, sir. They ran off towards the lake. I think they were going for a swim,' she said, looking shocked at her own embellishment. The Queen's Medal was hers for sure.

Miss Reedy approached Mr Plumpton. 'Josiah, may I have a word?'

The pair walked outside.

'I just heard Harry's announcement. Something must have happened. This isn't like that lot at all. Well, Sloane perhaps, and the old Jacinta, but the other four are very reliable. I'm worried. Millie abandoned Mrs Von Thripp quite some time ago and no one's seen Alice-Miranda since first thing this morning. I don't want to alarm anyone unnecessarily but I think you and I should go and see what we can find,' Miss Reedy suggested.

Josiah nodded.

Mr Lipp turned around to see the two teachers leaving.

'Where are they going?' he huffed. The Queen would be at the fair in just over two hours and he had hoped that the singers would have a wonderful first performance as their rehearsal. Blow the lot of them. He'd just have to make do. He gave Mr Trout a nod.

Chapter 38

Alice-Miranda took cover behind an old sideboard as she watched Donald Freeman turn the dial on the lock.

As he pulled on the door, he took a pen knife from his pocket with his other hand.

She wondered what to do next. She could run upstairs and call the police but she was more worried about what he planned to do with that knife. Surely he wouldn't destroy the art. That would be terrible.

Alice-Miranda scurried across the room and peered around the iron door. Mr Freeman wouldn't hurt her. He wasn't a killer.

Donald Freeman was standing in front of one of the paintings, the knife blade poised on the corner of the frame.

'Mr Freeman!' she cried out. 'Stop!'

From around the other side of the racks, a tall man with a shiny bald head rushed towards them. 'Well, well, well, what 'ave we got 'ere? Donny Freeman, you silly old coot. Put that knife away.'

Alice-Miranda backed up. She was ready to make a run for it.

Donald dropped the knife and it clattered to the ground. 'You! What are you doing here?' he asked the bald man.

'Takin' what belongs to a friend of ours. Along with a bit of interest. Nige'll be here shortly.' He looked over Donald's shoulder. 'And who are you, princess?'

'My name is Alice-Miranda Highton-Smith-Kennington-Jones,' she said defiantly. 'And you won't get away with this. It's Jezza, isn't it?'

The man's mouth gaped open. How on earth did she know his name?

Donald Freeman turned around as if registering for the first time that Alice-Miranda was even there.

'What are you going to do to stop us? You're knee high to a grasshopper. Don't think I won't hurt you if you try anything funny,' Jezza threatened.

Alice-Miranda ignored him and looked at Donald. 'Mr Freeman, I don't understand. Why? What were you going to do?'

Donald Freeman cupped his head in his hands. 'The paintings. The frames were too heavy. I was just going to take them upstairs and keep them safe . . .'

From the far side of the room came the sound of running feet.

'It's about time, Nige,' the tall man said. 'We've got visitors.'

'It's not Nigel,' Lucas shouted. Millie skidded in behind him, followed by Sep, Jacinta and Sloane. 'He's locked up. Same as you're going to be soon.'

Alice-Miranda smiled at her friends. 'Well done, Millie. They won't get away with it now.'

'I'll deal with you lot,' Jezza threatened. He looked at the children, then at the knife on the ground beside Donald, but Lucas saw it too.

'What have I done?' Mr Freeman gasped.

Quick as a flash, Lucas slid towards the pen knife and kicked it away. It clattered out of reach under one of the racks.

Jezza's eyes were wild. 'I'm not going back to prison,' he yelled. 'Not again! Get out of my way!'

Lucas got to his feet and together the children stood their ground.

'Mr Freeman, get out of here,' Alice-Miranda urged.

But the old man rushed towards Jezza and barged into him as hard as he could. The children rushed forward, pushing the thief into the cellar.

'Quickly,' Alice-Miranda urged. 'Help me!'

She, Lucas and Jacinta pulled on the vault door. Alice-Miranda spun the dial, trapping Jezza in the cellar with them. Donald Freeman collapsed onto a threadbare sofa in the corner, gasping for air.

'What are you doing?' Jezza growled as he regained his balance. 'Let me out of here.'

Alice-Miranda shook her head. 'You're not going anywhere.'

'What's the combination, you little brat?'

'As if she's going to tell you!' Jacinta yelled.

Alice-Miranda knew that if he couldn't get out through the vault he'd make a run for the cellar door. She motioned at Sep as if she was pushing something. He wondered what she was getting at until he spotted the giant beast on the other side of the room.

The lad raced towards the bear.

Jezza's eyes scanned the room. On the other side he spotted the door to freedom. He made a break for it.

But Sep was ready. The lad gave an almighty push and the polar bear began to wobble.

'Ahhhhh!' Jezza cried as the bear lunged towards him. 'Get away from me.' The beast crashed down, pinning the crook to the ground. 'Help me! Help!' Jezza wailed.

'Alice-Miranda, Millie, are you in there?' It was Miss Reedy on the other side of the vault door. Somehow she'd found the tunnel entrance.

Alice-Miranda ran to door and spun the dial.

Miss Reedy hurried out of the vault with Mr Plumpton behind her.

'Oh my heavens, what's going on?' the man cried. He spied Jezza's arms and legs flailing about underneath the bear. 'And who's that?'

Before the children could answer, the cellar door opened and revealed Fenella Freeman. 'What's all this?' she gasped.

Ed Clifton, Hugh Kennington-Jones and Cecelia Highton-Smith followed her.

'Daddy!' Alice-Miranda cried out and rushed over to embrace her parents and uncle. 'Mummy, how did you get them out of jail?'

'Get this thing off me!' Jezza yelled.

'Who *is* that?' Fenella demanded.

Alice-Miranda looked up at her. 'Detective Freeman, we know who stole the artworks.'

'What? How? It was your father and his brother. I know it was them.'

Cecelia eyeballed the woman. 'No, you don't, and that's why the judge gave them bail.'

'That man under Sidney works for Addison Goldsworthy. His name's Jezza and he's got an offsider called Nigel,' Alice-Miranda explained.

'And you'll find Nigel locked in the back of a truck by the summer house, along with a whole lot of paintings,' Sep added.

'They've been stealing paintings and bringing them here for storage. It's been happening for years,' said Alice-Miranda. 'There's a tunnel from the summer house and it leads into the vault.'

Fenella Freeman could hardly believe the tale. And it was about to get a whole lot worse.

Over in the corner, Donald Freeman stood up from the sofa.

Fenella covered her mouth. 'Dad, what are you doing down here?'

The old man hesitated. 'It was me, Fen,' he said, his voice trembling. 'I started it.'

The children and adults walked towards him.

'What? What are you talking about?' asked Fenella.

'Years ago, when one of my clients couldn't afford to pay me, he said he'd do whatever he could do. Well, he had a Turner. That's what he could do. And then there was a Constable and a Monet and there were ten in all. Ten works I adored.' The old man's eyes filled with tears. 'I told you I'd own them one day.'

'How could you?' Fenella demanded. She ran towards him. Ed caught her before she could inflict her wrath. 'But why were they here? How?' she cried.

Alice-Miranda rushed to the man's side. Donald gulped.

Fenella took a deep breath. 'Now, I see. This is why you wanted to live at Pelham Park?'

Donald nodded. 'I could come and see my paintings any time I wanted.'

'But how did you know about the vault?' Hugh asked.

Alice-Miranda answered for him. 'It was Grandpa, wasn't it? He was your friend, the one you called Harry. His name was Henry but Harry must have been his nickname as a boy. He was the one who showed you how to get in and out of the house.'

'I don't understand how Addison Goldsworthy fits into the picture. How did he know about the vault too?' asked Cee.

'Nigel and Jezza used to make deliveries for me. When I retired, they went to work elsewhere. Goldsworthy must have had the same sort of needs,' Donald Freeman said slowly. 'I imagine they just kept bringing things here for storage. I wondered why there were paintings I couldn't quite place – I just thought it was my mind playing tricks on me.' The old man brushed the tears from his eyes.

Alice-Miranda reached out to hold his wrinkled hand. 'You took the blame, didn't you?'

'The blame for what?' Fenella demanded. She was completely confused.

'You and Grandpa Henry were great friends but then Grandpa shot his father's prized stallion by accident, didn't he?' Alice-Miranda began. 'And he made you take the blame. You went to a boys' home and your father was dismissed from his position as the butler.'

'What are you talking about?' Fenella gasped. She'd never heard any of this before.

Cecelia could barely believe her ears either. 'But darling, how did you know that?'

'I found Mr Freeman's father's employment records in the attic when Uncle Ed and I were looking for the receipts. Part of the record was missing and I knew something wasn't right. When Mr Freeman was upset earlier in the week, he had remembered something. He said that it wasn't his fault. That Harry had made him do it.'

'I'm still here if you haven't noticed, being squashed by a ten-tonne bear,' Jezza moaned.

'Put a sock in it,' Ed snapped.

'It still doesn't explain why you stored the art here,' Hugh said, turning back to Donald.

'I always thought that if it was found, your father would get the blame. After what he did, that was fine by me. But then when he died, I just left it here. I had nowhere else to keep it. When the house was transformed, and I got the chance to come and live here, it was perfect. I came down almost every night.

I could see my beautiful paintings. Before then, I used to park by the summer house and sneak in after dark. But I was getting much too old for that.'

'Surely you knew that we'd find them one day,' said Hugh.

'I thought I'd be dead by then. But when Alice-Miranda told me your brother was here and then Fen mentioned the Turner, I knew I couldn't leave them any longer. If I let you take the blame then I'd be no better than your father. I was going to take them upstairs last night and hide them in my apartment but I couldn't lift them in their frames. I was going to leave you this when I died, so you'd know what to do with them.' Donald pulled a small leather-bound book from his trouser pocket. Hugh reached forward and took it.

'That's why you had the knife,' Alice-Miranda said.

Hugh scanned the first two pages. It was a full confession as well as Donald's wishes that all of the paintings be returned to the galleries from which they'd been stolen.

Hugh sucked air between his teeth. 'This *is* a revelation.'

Donald stared at his daughter. His seawater-green eyes clouded over. 'I'm sorry, Fen. Is your mum home yet? School's out early again.'

Alice-Miranda looked at the man in confusion.

'I'm so sorry. I'll pack Dad's things tonight,' said Fenella, fighting back tears. 'He'll be charged, of course.'

Hugh shook his head. 'Please don't do that. Your father has a home here for as long as he wants one.'

Alice-Miranda rushed over to her father and threw her arms around his waist. 'Thank you, Daddy.'

'I don't know what to say,' Fenella breathed. 'Thank you, Mr Kennington-Jones.' She turned to her father. 'Come on, Dad. I'll get you upstairs and you can have a lie down.'

Mr Plumpton looked at his watch and cleared his throat. 'Right. Well, I'm sure that by now Mr Lipp has lost his mind over you lot going missing from the choir. Perhaps we should get back outside and try to enjoy the rest of the afternoon? Queen Georgiana will be coming shortly so, Miss Reedy, you'll need some time to get the rest of those awards sorted.'

Miss Reedy nodded, and Alice-Miranda and her father led the group out of the cellar.

'Still here,' Jezza moaned.

'Don't worry, old chap. Someone will be back to get you soon,' said Ed. He closed the cellar door and turned the key in the lock.

Chapter 39

As expected, Harold Lipp exploded like a firecracker when he saw the children and adults appear. 'Where have you lot been?'

Miss Reedy glowered at him. 'They have been with us. And any further information is on a need-to-know basis. *You* don't need to know.'

'What?' Harold huffed.

'Sorry, Mr Lipp,' Alice-Miranda apologised. 'But we're here now and I think Aunty Gee is on her way.'

The whump of a helicopter rotor had indeed filled the air.

'Places everyone. Don't let me down. Thank heavens for Caprice. She's been my saving grace this afternoon.' He beamed at the child and wrinkled his lip at the others.

But Caprice was annoyed. It didn't look as if Alice-Miranda and her friends were in trouble at all.

The rest of the students, residents and guests jammed into the marquee to await Her Majesty's arrival.

There was a collective gasp and spontaneous round of applause as Queen Georgiana entered the tea marquee flanked by her personal bodyguard, Dalton, and her lady-in-waiting, Mrs Marmalade.

'Hello everyone,' the Queen called. 'How lovely to be here. I trust you're having a wonderful day.'

'Hello Aunty Gee.' Cecelia rushed forward and gave the woman a hug.

Her Majesty studied her god-daughter's face. 'Are you all right, darling?'

'I'll tell you all about it in a moment. I think the children are going to perform for you first.'

'Oh, lovely.' Aunty Gee looked up at the choir and smiled. Alice-Miranda and Millie were standing front and centre. She gave them a wave. 'Hello darlings.'

Matron Bright approached and nervously directed the Queen to her seat at the ornately decorated table closest to the stage.

Mr Trout glanced at Mr Lipp, who held his hands aloft ready to start. Mr Trout began his extravagant introduction on the keyboard and Caprice's angelic voice rang out.

'Oh my goodness, she's a talent,' Mr Mobbs said loudly.

'What? I can't hear anything,' yelled Mr Johnson.

'Turn up your hearing aid, you silly old coot.' Mr Mobbs made a twisting motion near his ear.

The children joined in with the chorus and finished their first song to a rousing ovation.

After five more tunes they completed their set and Caprice stepped forward to take a bow.

Miss Grimm walked towards the stage and spotted Miss Reedy off to the side.

'Has it all gone well?' Miss Grimm whispered pointedly. She was wondering why she hadn't been able to find Miss Reedy earlier.

'Let's just say we had an unexpected adventure,' the English teacher murmured back. She handed the headmistress a sheet of paper. 'These are the Queen's Blue recipients and the winner of the medal.'

'This is a surprise,' Miss Grimm remarked as she scanned the page and approached the microphone. The choir was still standing in their position on stage.

Caprice had been listening to the teachers' conversation, her heart pounding. She was about to receive a medal from the Queen herself.

'Thank you, Mr Lipp and the Winchester-Fayle Singers. That was a truly delightful performance. Stunning,' Miss Grimm began, and led another round of applause. 'Good afternoon, everyone. My name is Ophelia Grimm and I am the headmistress of Winchesterfield-Downsfordvale Academy for Proper Young Ladies. On behalf of Professor Winterbottom at Fayle School for Boys and myself, I would like to thank the staff and residents of Bagley Hall and Pelham Park for being part of our camp week. Some of you may not be aware that we have been trialling a new youth-award system for Her Majesty. From all reports it's been a wonderful experience and one that our students won't soon forget. So may I invite Queen Georgiana to the stage to announce the names of the students who will receive the newly founded award, the Queen's Blue, which is the first level of a broader scheme called the Queen's Colours.'

Queen Georgiana approached the stage.

'Oh, I told you I liked her,' Mr Mobbs said. 'That's a good-looking woman.'

Mrs Marmalade turned and scowled.

Queen Georgiana thanked a raft of people before she looked down at the awards list. Her forehead creased and she looked up at the teachers. 'Do you mean to tell me . . .?'

Miss Reedy nodded.

'Good heavens! Well, my life has just been made very easy.' Queen Georgiana grinned. 'There's no need to read a long list of names . . . every single child has achieved their Blue. Well done to all of you.'

A cheer went up from the children. Millie looked at Alice-Miranda. Both girls were stunned. They were sure they'd missed out after all the disasters they'd had.

Caprice was far less impressed. 'What? But that's impossible. Alice-Miranda messed up lots of things.'

Miss Reedy glared at the girl from the side of the stage.

Queen Georgiana's eyes flicked to Caprice for a split second, and then she spoke again. 'I do, however, have the honour of reading one name. The winner of the Queen's Medal for outstanding all-round qualities is . . .' She paused for effect.

Caprice was listening. She closed her eyes and heard her name. 'Me!' she yelled and stepped forward.

'Not unless your name is Septimus Sykes, dear,' Queen Georgiana announced.

Caprice looked set to erupt. 'What? It can't be him!'

Sep strode over to Her Majesty.

There was a loud cheer from the other students as the boy shook Queen Georgiana's hand.

'This is not happening!' Caprice screamed. 'That's my medal. I earned it. You don't know what I had to make Millie do to stop *her* from winning it.' She pointed at Alice-Miranda. 'Give me that medal!' Caprice rushed at Sep and snatched the award from the boy's hand.

'Excuse me, young lady.' Queen Georgiana promptly snatched it back, then turned to Miss Reedy and Miss Grimm. 'Perhaps you might like to rethink the awarding of a complete set of Blues?'

'Caprice, sit down now,' the English teacher barked at the child.

'She might sing like an angel and look like one too, but that's where the resemblance stops,' Mr Mobbs called out.

Queen Georgiana arched her eyebrow. 'I quite agree.'

Caprice stormed off the stage and stomped out of the marquee.

Mr Lipp ran after her. 'Caprice, come back. We know you didn't mean it . . .'

Mr Plumpton and Miss Reedy stared at each other, goggle-eyed. It seemed that Caprice had saved her most impressive performance until the very end.

'Oh dear, I think I owe Millie an apology,' Mr Plumpton whispered. 'And Alice-Miranda.'

Miss Reedy nodded. 'Yes, me too.'

Alice-Miranda and Millie looked at each other. They hadn't needed to do a thing about Caprice Radford. She had brought herself well and truly unstuck.

Millie squeezed Alice-Miranda's hand. 'Well, that was a surprise.'

'I think there's been a few of those today.' Alice-Miranda grinned and squeezed Millie's hand right back.

And just in case you're wondering . . .

Donald Freeman had indeed been Henry Kennington-Jones's best friend. One dreary winter's afternoon Henry, or Harry, as he was then known, had convinced Donald to go shooting with him. They were after pheasant or rabbits but Henry had terrible aim. After one particularly wild shot, the boys heard a sickening thud. They ran towards the sound and found Henry's father's prize stallion dead. Henry handed Donald the gun just as the young stablehand arrived to bring the beast in for the night.

Henry ran and left Donald holding the evidence. The boy was blamed for the horse's death and his father was dismissed from Pelham Park. But worse was still to come. Donald was sent to a home for delinquent boys. He never got over being blamed for a crime he didn't commit. As far as Donald knew, rich people could do anything and get away with it. Donald's love of art blossomed a few years later when, to appease his guilt, Henry had sent the young man an artwork from the house with a note instructing him to sell it and make a better life for himself.

Donald fell in love with the picture, a Turner. But in the end he sold it on the black market to fund his studies. He always hoped he'd get it back again one day but he didn't know how. When one of his clients couldn't pay a bill, he offered him an artwork instead. It was that very same Turner that came back to him. Over the years Donald received more stolen works and stored them in the cellars at Highton Hall, knowing that if they were found, the blame would fall on Henry Kennington-Jones. It seemed only fair.

Fenella had no choice but to charge Donald with receiving stolen goods. He was placed on a lengthy good behaviour bond. Hugh Kennington-Jones vouched for the man, just as he had promised.

The judge considered Donald's age and state of mind and decided that a stint in prison was not in anyone's best interests.

The artworks were returned to their owners, including Ed Clifton's painting, which went back to its home at the Metropolitan Museum of Art in New York. It was a mere coincidence that Addison Goldsworthy had received that painting last of all.

Nigel and Jezza were charged with theft and numerous other crimes. They confessed all, which turned out to be a far bigger case than the one against Donald Freeman. The night before the fair, just as they were depositing Ed Clifton's stolen painting, they'd received instructions to remove everything from the vault the next day and meet a ship that was sailing for Russia. Addison Goldsworthy had done the biggest deal of his life with a treacherous oligarch called Boris Karlovsky, but instead of receiving a fortune he earned himself several more years in prison.

Fenella was promoted, however, she requested her transfer be put on hold for a little while so she could stay close to her ailing father.

Ed Clifton made peace with Pelham Park and her ghosts. He visited his parents' grave and laid flowers for his mother. He thought that next time he came home, he might stay at Highton Hall instead – surely he'd have a quieter time there.

Caprice Radford lost her Queen's Blue. Miss Grimm met with her parents and, despite Caprice throwing the most enormous tantrum and demanding to be expelled, the adults decided that she should stay on at Winchesterfield-Downsfordvale. Her parents couldn't have been more grateful to Miss Grimm for keeping her at the school. Miss Reedy questioned Millie and Alice-Miranda but neither girl said anything about Caprice's manipulations. They had both decided not to make her life any harder than it was set to become. Caprice was in enough trouble as it was.

Apart from a few pieces that Hugh and Ed kept for themselves, the rest of Arabella Kennington-Jones's art collection was sold off. The money would ensure Pelham Park would exist for a very long time to come.

Aunty Gee was thrilled to roll out her Queen's Colours program around the country and had already started devising the next level. She thought Plum had a nice ring to it.

Cast of characters

The Highton-Smith-Kennington-Jones family

Cecelia Highton-Smith	Alice-Miranda's mother
Hugh Kennington-Jones	Alice-Miranda's father
Ed Clifton	Hugh's brother

Winchesterfield-Downsfordvale Academy for Proper Young Ladies staff

Miss Ophelia Grimm	Headmistress
Aldous Grump	Miss Grimm's husband
Mrs Louella Derby	Personal Secretary to the headmistress
Miss Livinia Reedy	English teacher
Mr Josiah Plumpton	Science teacher
Miss Benitha Wall	PE teacher
Howie (Mrs Howard)	Housemistress
Shaker (Mrs Shakeshaft)	Assistant housemistress
Mr Cornelius Trout	Music teacher
Mrs Doreen Smith	Cook
Charlie Weatherly (Mr Charles)	Gardener

Winchesterfield-Downsfordvale students

Alice-Miranda Highton-Smith-Kennington-Jones	
Millicent Jane McLoughlin-McTavish-McNoughton-McGill	Alice-Miranda's best friend and room mate
Jacinta Headlington-Bear	Friend
Sloane Sykes	Friend
Caprice Radford	New student
Susannah Dare, Danika Rigby, Shelby Shore	Friends

Fayle School for Boys staff and students

Professor Winterbottom	Headmaster
Mr Harold Lipp	English and Drama teacher
Septimus Sykes	A student and Sloane Sykes's brother
Lucas Nixon, George 'Figgy' Figworth, Rufus Pemberley	Students

Other

Matron Bright	Manages Pelham Park aged care home
Donald Freeman	Resident of Pelham Park
Detective Sergeant Fenella Freeman	Local police officer and daughter of Donald Freeman
Beth, Lionel	Instructors at Bagley Hall camp
Jezza, Nigel	Criminals